Angel
Academy

Angel Academy Book 1

KATE HALL

Lost Window LLC

"I am a being of Heaven and Earth, of thunder and lightning, of rain and wind, of the galaxies."
Eden Ahbez

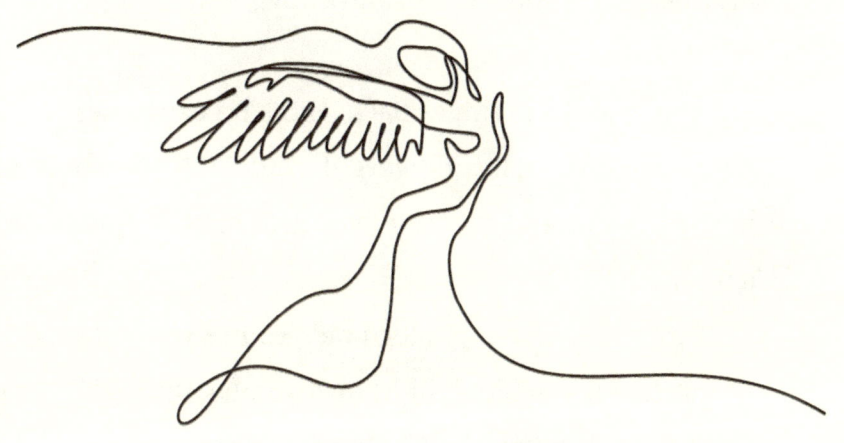

Chapter One

Discovering that there really is an afterlife is sort of jarring.

The last sound I ever hear should be the screeching of metal, the shattering of glass, but it's not. The only sound on Earth is Desireé's heartbeat. But then, she dies, and I die with her.

I expect it to be dark, or, more accurately, for there to be nothing. After all, I've never believed in the whole "life after death" thing. It's just a fairy-tale meant to make people feel better, isn't it? Instead, I'm lying in a field, holding her hand. None of that death stuff seems too important. She's here, and her expression is so full of love that I might burst.

I smile, and she smiles back, and a breeze blows over us, ruffling the flowers. I could fall asleep here for days, and I let my eyes drift shut for just a moment.

"I love you, Avery." Her voice comes to me in wisps, like it's made of light instead of sound. My lips tilt up, but I'm just too tired to open my eyes or reply.

When she removes her hand from mine, though, my eyes snap open.

The field is gone, and so is the breeze, and so is she.

Her name, I think. What was her name? I grind my teeth, and tears prick at my eyes. She's not here with me, so of course it matters.

The ceiling is high above me, built from intricate white marble that glitters in the golden light. I blink, but the brightness doesn't dissipate. I glance down. I'm in a bed with white sheets. A hospital bed?

"Avery," a voice says to my left. I turn my head, and a woman is standing beside me in a knee-length gown of the palest blue, like a summer sky turned to fabric. I want to touch it to see what it's made of, but my hands won't obey.

"Where am I?" I ask. There's no way I would have ended up in the fanciest hospital in the world, not in my tiny town on the coast of Oregon. This place is grand, fit for a queen. Or a goddess.

The meadow girl's face is beginning to fade from my memory, the brightness of this place drowning it out. I grasp desperately at it, but it's like trying to contain smoke.

"You're in the hospital wing at Theaa Academy. You were brought in this morning," the woman says slowly, her voice light as silver bells. Her brown hair is up in a loose bun, small wisps falling to frame her face perfectly.

"I've never heard of it," I say, sitting up slowly. I don't have any soreness, but that could be a trick of the medication. Except, when I look at my arms, there are no tubes or wires. If I'm in a hospital, shouldn't I be hurt? The memory of shattering glass is somewhere in the depths of my mind, just barely within reach. Did I manage to escape injury?

Whatever Theaa Academy is, though, it must be private and expensive. The room I'm in is old-fashioned, a medical wing from a movie set in the past. Each bed has a curtain that can be pulled around it, but I seem to be the only person here right now. Well, besides the woman. Is she a nurse? A doctor?

She tilts her head, a kind smile crossing her face. I want to crawl into her arms like I used to do with Mom when I was little. That's ridiculous, though. I don't even know this woman.

But, somehow, I feel almost like I do.

Almost.

"Avery, what is your last memory?"

I open my mouth to tell her about the meadow, but it's like my tongue is glued down. I can't speak. I'm not...supposed to? That seems correct, although it doesn't make sense. I close my mouth again and go through my mind, starting at the beginning of yesterday.

"I was at school. No, driving after. It had been a bad day, and I wasn't paying enough attention in the rain. The car lost traction around a curve, and..." There had been a scream, an impact of some sort, but then what? I rack my mind for what happened next, but the images won't come.

"It's okay," the woman says, sitting gently on the side of the bed. She rests a hand on my knee. I don't usually like touching, but she's warm, like coming home to a cozy fireplace. "You might never remember. That's normal."

"Did I hit my head?" I ask, twining my hands together.

Her eyes go sad, and she pulls her hand away.

"Avery," she says carefully, as if testing my name on her tongue, although she's said it so many times already. "You are no longer on Earth."

The words don't make sense. I bark out a short, sharp laugh. "What, am I on Mars or something?"

She smiles, but the motion doesn't reach her eyes. Why isn't she laughing? It had been a joke, obviously.

Right?

My face falls. My throat tightens. "Where am I?" I ask quietly. Fear grips my heart like a vice.

She doesn't answer for a moment, instead taking the time to unwrap my taut hands from each other so that she can take both of them in hers. Her pale brown eyes bore into mine, almost as if she's searching for something.

Finally, she says, "You're in Heaven, Avery."

"Heaven?" I gasp out after sitting there for far too long. This has to be some sort of joke. I didn't die. There's no way. Maybe it's a dream. I bark out a laugh at the absurd statement. Heaven isn't even real.

I look around the room once again, then down at my hands. Nothing has changed. I remember reading that I should check the time twice to see if it changes during a dream, but there are no clocks in this room, and my phone is nowhere in sight. In fact, the whole place looks like it's straight out of the forties.

The woman nods sagely. "I know this may be difficult to process, but it's the truth. Yesterday at four thirty-six in the afternoon, in Brookstown,

Washington, the vehicle you were driving went off the road and into the river. You and one other passenger were killed on impact.

I open my mouth, then close it again. I should feel sad, panicked, even. Instead, an irresistible calm washes over me. I'm dead, and there's nothing I can do about it. And now I'm in Heaven. Actual Heaven.

Okay, then.

"What about..." I search for the name of the passenger, any memory of who could have been in the car with me, but it doesn't come to me. It's like a censor blur has been placed over them completely.

Her face falls. "I'm afraid that she was not as lucky as you."

I bite my lip. I feel a little bad about the whole situation, but I can't even picture who died with me. That should make me feel worse, but instead, I just feel distant. Who knows, maybe it had been a hitchhiker that decided to kill us both by making me swerve off the cliff. It's probably best not to dwell on it.

Instead, I ask, "Who are you, anyway?"

The woman's face brightens by several degrees. "My name is Azrael. I am the Dean of Theaa Academy."

I tilt my head. The name definitely rings a bell. "Wait. Azrael, as in…"

She nods. "Yes, I've been mentioned in a few notable books in the past."

An angel. I'm having a conversation with a freaking angel.

I stand up carefully, although there's no need. I feel better than I've felt in years. No hunger pangs in my stomach, and my once bad ankle isn't sore at all.

"Wow," I mutter, looking over myself. I'm wearing a flowing white linen gown with gold stitched into the fibers, and it hangs off my shoulders elegantly. The blonde hair that floats around me is paler than before, nearly as white as the marble room, and it's practically glowing.

Azrael gives me an amused smile. "Just wait until you get your wings."

I freeze and stare at her, my eyes practically popping out of my head.

"Wings?"

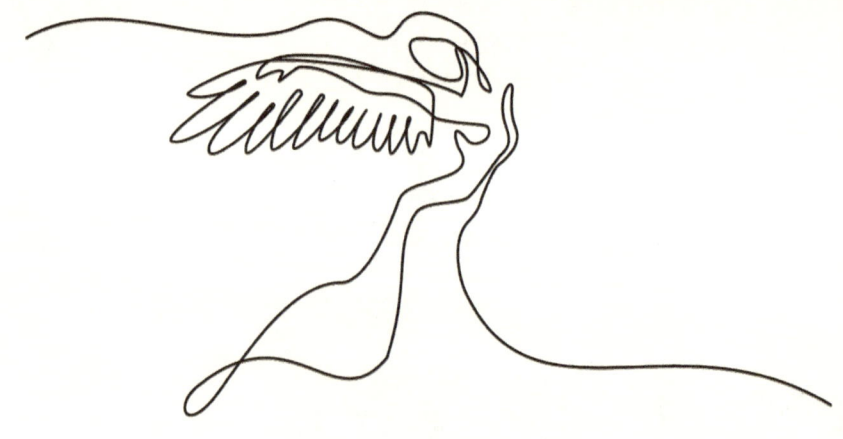

Chapter Two

Azrael doesn't explain the wing comment, merely winks and leads me out of the great marble hall. When we leave the room, we enter another area, this one a walkway over a sheer sparkling mountain. Waterfalls cascade down with no apparent source, the water glistening in golden light. The stone we step on shines and sparkles like it's made of diamonds.

It might be.

Because this is Heaven.

For real.

"This is one of the many quarters of Heaven,"

Azrael explains, extending an arm outward. I look past the mist and clouds, squinting until I can just make out another mountain in the distance. Whatever is on top is a shining gold, like something out of a fairytale.

"Wow," I whisper, leaning out over the marble rail that extends from the floor up to an open-air window, pillars every few feet to form several elegant arches. "This is unreal."

This definitely isn't a fancy hospital. These places don't exist in real life.

"I assure you," Azrael says gently, "this is all quite real."

I sigh and follow her, my head swiveling side to side.

"I'll be taking you to your room first," she says. "You'll want to get changed in time for dinner."

"Dinner?" I ask. "Aren't we, like, immortal beings or something?"

She shrugs. "Eating may not be necessary to sustain us, but it's a pleasant time that we like to use to help you all come together at the end of a long day of training."

I frown. "Why do we need training? Isn't there a way you could just…" I wiggle my fingers in front of my face. "Matrix the information we need into our heads?"

She watches me for a moment. "Our Creator still insists that all previous humans be imbued with free will. We do not give you anything you do not already have."

I nod. I guess that sort of makes sense, but it would be much cooler if the information I'm supposed to learn were just siphoned into my head.

We end up in another grand hall nearly identical to the first, except this one is lined with dark wooden tables instead of hospital beds. I look up, but the ceiling isn't a starry sky like in my favorite book series. Oh, well.

A few other people are in this room, reading from books or eating food or just hanging out. There's one notable thing about all of them, though. They're all teenagers, most with glowing white wings, and a few without. A few look up and smile at me, and one, a girl with strawberry blonde hair and iridescent white wings tucked against her back, gives me a little wave. I wave back, although I feel exposed in the long white gown instead of the navy blue school uniforms they all appear to be wearing. This dress may be magical and elegant, but it also stands in stark contrast to everyone else.

I chew on my lip for a moment.

"Why is —" but I'm cut off before I can complete the thought.

"Azrael," a young man calls. His hair is a pale brown, his skin is dark as night, and his wings stand out brighter than the sun. Does nobody here have dark hair? Maybe it's a Heaven thing. I study Azrael, whose darker brown hair is completely different to the students. I'll have to ask someone about that.

We stop, and I wrap my arms around myself. I am not wearing a bra, and I'm suddenly very self-conscious about it. I've never gone anywhere without one, and now I'm flitting around like a lost fairy princess with far too flimsy apparel.

"Yes, Gabriel?" she asks, lifting her chin.

Gabriel like the archangel?

"I needed some help with my theory homework. Will you be returning to normal office hours tomorrow?"

She nods, a soft smile on her face. "I will also be available as soon as I finish showing Avery around. She's a new student."

The boy turns to me, and his face lights up with a grin. He sticks a hand out. "Hi, I'm Gabriel, but everyone calls me Gabe. Not the famous Gabriel, though." He laughs at his own words and rolls his eyes. Well, at least I have an answer to one of my many questions. "That one teaches fencing."

Fencing?

I consider his words as he says goodbye. That's two archangels from theology. Will I be meeting others? I try to remember their names from the very small amount of church I attended as a young child, but I only know the names of Azrael and Gabriel from TV shows. Is Metatron a real one, or was he just made up for that show? It sounds fake, so I can't be sure. I frown.

"I know it's a lot to take in," Azrael says, placing a soft hand on my shoulder. "Don't worry, you will fit in well when you get used to being here.

You must have been extraordinary in life to make it here. The Creator doesn't take this responsibility lightly. They only choose the best of the best for our purposes."

I nod gravely and follow her. We walk up a spiral marble staircase to a long hallway.

I sigh. It's going to take forever to get to where we need to go.

Azrael smiles deviously. "Would you like to see something cool?"

I'm a bit concerned about what an ancient being might consider "cool." I'm not sure what else I can handle today, but I nod.

"Two hundred twenty-three," Azrael says, knocking three times on the unlabeled door directly to the right of us. Slowly, golden numbers become visible. Two hundred twenty-three. "We try to make life easy for our students," Azrael says. She opens the door, but I'm almost afraid to look in. Will I have a roommate? Is the room frightening and foreign? Does it look like a magical palace bedroom from a movie? She smiles at me and puts a finger under my chin so that I look into her eyes.

"Avery, everything is going to be okay."

When I walk through the door, I gasp.

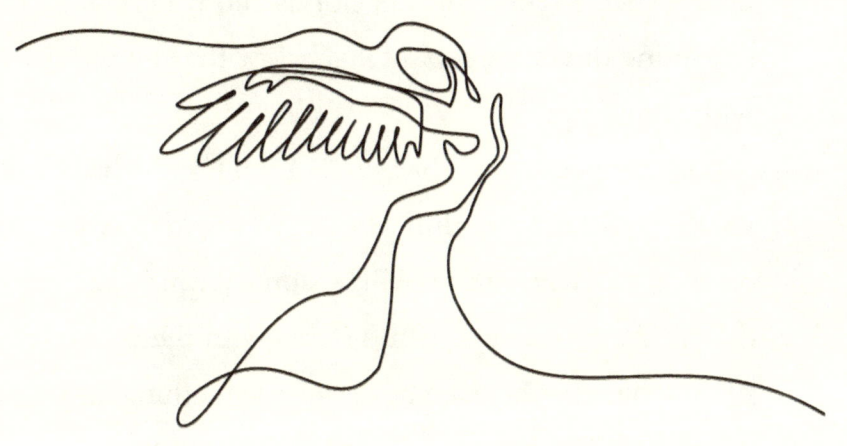

Chapter Three

"It's...mine," I say.

The room is my room from back home. There's my bed in the corner, but it's about twice the size of my usual cramped twin. There are posters and paintings on the wall, almost all gifts from friends and family. The ugly crack in the wall is gone, and so are the mold-scented water stains in the ceiling. The bile-yellow wall is now a more pale shade that's light and airy, and the desk in the corner is the fancy one I kept looking at online for college, but in its essence, it's my room. Instead of a field of rusting cars and tall grass, the window reveals a scenic view of clouds and waterfalls streaming down the mountains below the shining white building.

"If you want any changes," Azrael says, her voice careful once again, "you only have to focus on what you want, and it will be done. We just find that students are more comfortable with the transition when they're encompassed in something familiar.

I take a step inside, my mouth agape. My fingers trace over the footboard, then the lamp in the corner.

"So if I wanted it to be bigger, or the floor to be hardwood...?" I ask, turning back to the angel in the doorway.

She nods. "Anything you'd like."

I picture the floor as hardwood, but I also consider what it would be like for it to be heated, and it changes immediately. My bare feet are heated on the dark, warm wood, and I smile to myself.

"I'm going to give you some time alone," she says. "You will be notified when it's time for dinner. There are proper clothes in your closet. If there is anything you need, you only need to focus on it."

I nod, but I'm not paying much attention at this point. What more could I possibly need in this place? A sleeve of Oreos, maybe, but nothing else. When I glance back at the desk, there's a pristine new package of Oreos resting on the white wood.

The door closes as Azrael leaves, and I take the Oreos and collapse on the bed. Should I be crying? I am dead, after all. But I can't summon tears, or even sadness for that matter. I may be dead, but I'm in Heaven. Freaking Heaven. My heart races with elation. Of all the people in the world, I'm one of the ones that made it to Heaven.

I sit up and put an Oreo to my mouth, but then, the question that's been niggling in my mind finally comes to the forefront.

Why is there a school in Heaven?

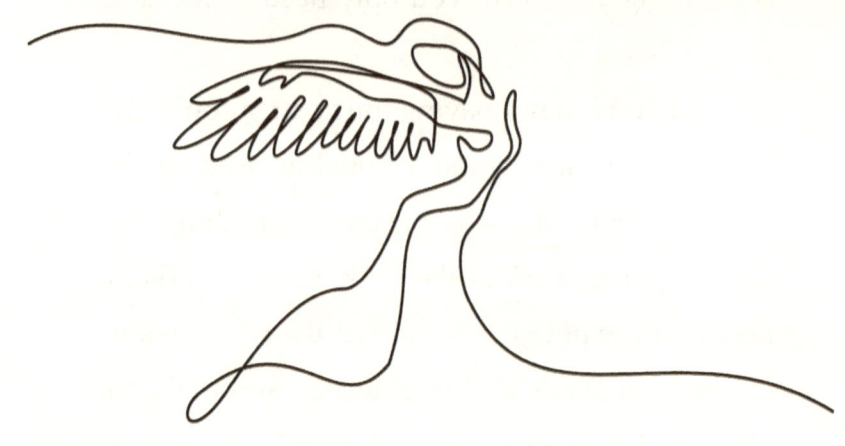

Chapter Four

A gentle bell rings at the door right as I finish getting changed, and I check myself in the door's mirror, which is cleaner than the one at home, but otherwise identical. I look like me, but different. More. My skin is clear and luminescent, not a red blotch or pimple in sight, and my hair is so much paler than the dirty blonde it used to be. Instead of being a frizzy mess of split-ends, it falls in the gentle waves I would've had on Earth had I been able to afford the fancy shampoos and conditioners needed for it.

I test my weight on my once bad foot again.

When I was twelve, I broke my ankle, and it's never been the same since my parents couldn't afford to take me to the hospital. After years of constant pain, it's like I've been given a whole new foot. I didn't realize how much it used to hurt until the pain just...stopped. Because of that alone, my whole body is a million times lighter.

I sigh and open the door. There are a few others in the hall, and I follow them down the same spiral staircase from earlier. I still get a few glances, but less than when I walked into the cafeteria with my white gown on. At least now I match everyone else.

"Avery," a familiar voice says. Gabe's arm loops through mine. "It's good to see you again! How are you adjusting to Theaa Academy?" He's smiling once again. Or is it still? How much does he smile?

I smile back warily. "It's...a lot," I admit. At least he seems friendly.

He nods. "Yeah, it was for me, too when I first showed up." He pauses and looks at me. "What brought you here? For me it was cancer."

My eyes widen. "I'm so sorry," I say. What else is there to say?

He laughs. "It's alright. We end up talking about that sort of thing a lot around here. It can be hard to remember pieces of your old life, and even harder to find something in common. Cause of death is an easy one."

Holy crap, that's morbid for Heaven.

Although, we are dead. It makes sense that death would be brought up.

I open my mouth, close it again, then finally say, "I was in a car accident. Drove off a ravine."

This time, he's the one who looks shocked. "Wow. That's wild. Most people are pretty standard." He taps on a girl's shoulder, and she glances back at us. It's the girl with the strawberry blonde hair that had waved at me earlier. "Huỳnh here had a stroke." He pronounces her name like "Win," but breathier and sort of monotone, and I commit it to memory.

I gasp. "But you're so young!"

She laughs. "Everyone looks young here. I was eighty-five when I died."

So that explains one thing—why everyone here is a teenager—but nothing else. Like the reason that there is a school in Heaven. It doesn't make any sense. I nod at her like I understand.

Gabe points a finger at me enthusiastically. "Gruesome car wreck!"

Huỳnh nods, but she doesn't seem as excited as Gabe. "He's always like this," she says. "Can't put him in a bad mood."

He laughs. "Why would I be? I'm seventeen, I'm in freaking Heaven, and I get unlimited food. With only one *minor* downside, what is there to be unhappy about?"

Huỳnh rolls her eyes. "Do you want to sit with us in the mess?" she asks, her eyes trained back on me every few seconds as she watches her path down the stairs. I look between them, then nod.

Just as I'm about to ask about the downside that Gabe mentioned, we walk into the grand mess hall from earlier and take our seats. Huỳnh places a finger over her lips and points at the front of the room just as I'm about to open my mouth to ask my question. Okay, then.

Azrael is at the podium, her wings spread high in an elegant arc behind her. "Welcome to a new term at Theaa Academy," she says. Her voice is conversational, like she's just talking to me, but it carries throughout the entire hall somehow. That's a neat trick. "We are pleased to welcome several new students, and we hope that you will all find your place in our esteemed program. Now, I'm not one for speeches, so thank you for your brief attention, and enjoy your meal."

As food appears in front of me, I look around. There are a few others at my table with the same confused expression I must be sporting. At least I'm not the only one.

"It's an interesting coincidence that I…" I don't want to use the word "died," so I say, "showed up at the beginning of term."

Huỳnh looks up from her plate, some sort of noodle meal with what appears to be chicken on top and a yellow sauce, chopped green ovens over it all. "It's not. Time isn't linear, so all new students arrive at the beginning of a new term. There are usually about fifty new people, and then the rest of us."

"Oh," I say, looking down at my plate, and my mouth instantly waters. It's baked parmesan, and I lean over and breathe in. Sure enough, the fried bit on top is not chicken, but Pacific salmon. My favorite. "How do they do all this?"

Gabe shrugs. "Nobody really knows, but who cares?" He bites into a spring roll, and I smile before diving into my own meal.

I could get used to this place. After eating, we head back upstairs, and students spread out to the nearest doorways, each whispering a number and walking in, one after the other. The further the hall goes, the fewer students, but every door appears capable of this incredible feat. I smile at the little bit of magic.

Gabe stands at the door next to mine, and I catch him before he enters. "What are we supposed to do all night?" I ask.

He shrugs. "Whatever you want. Sleep, watch movies, learn about the secrets of the universe… It's pretty much free time until class starts in the morning."

I nod. "And what are—" I try to ask, but he's gone.

I frown before entering my room. There's not much to do but sleep, so I open the dresser to find my favorite pair of pajamas, except they're in pristine condition, just like the rest of the room. When I frown at their too-new shape, though, they begin to look just a bit more worn. Not as bad as the ones back home, but more familiar.

Much better.

When I collapse into my perfectly comfortable bed, I fall into an immediate, dreamless sleep.

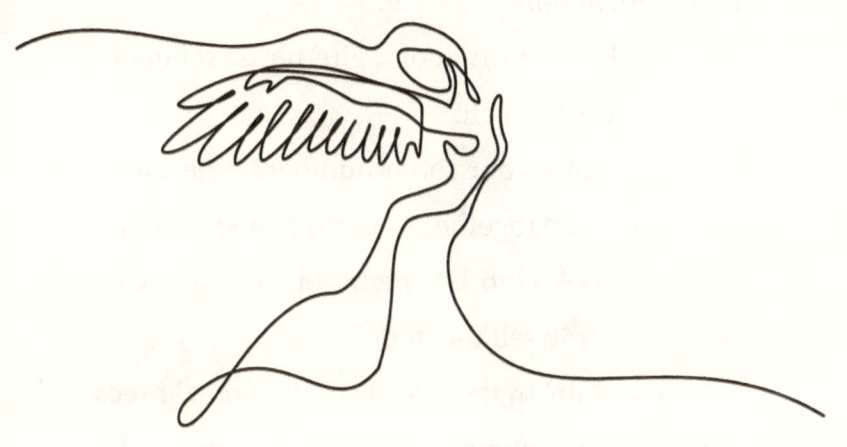

Chapter Five

The same gentle bell alarm as yesterday wakes me. I'm almost convinced it was all a dream, but when I glance out the window, I'm greeted by the breathtaking sight of the mountain that the school sits atop. Will I ever get used to this view?

I don't have to stretch after waking up—I'm not even drowsy. I was asleep, and now I'm not. There doesn't seem to be an in-between. It's almost like I just laid down. My navy uniform is gone from the floor, and when I open my closet, it's hanging up. Instead of the ugly uniform loafers that I wore last night, though, there are a pair of black boots. I smile. Much more my style.

As I'm leaving my room, Huỳnh is coming out of hers across the hall.

"Hey, what's your room number?" she asks as we fall into step together. "I thought about inviting you for a book club last night, but I didn't know your number to tell the door."

A book club? In the middle of the night? I recall what Gabe said about night being free time. "Two twenty-three," I say. Spending time with other students could be good for me. I feel super out of place.

"We're reading Jane Austen. She wrote something new and wanted us to read it." I gape. Again. I have to keep my jaw shut, or I'll begin to look like I don't actually know how to close my mouth.

"That sounds fun," I manage. Trying way to hard to be casual, I ask, "Is she, um, a student here?"

Huỳnh laughs, and I look at the ground. "No, but I met her at a book shop recently and we got to talking."

Book shops in Heaven? I would love to see one.

We make our way downstairs, and I'm caught

on the arm by Azrael. "I'm in a hurry," she says slowly, "but I wanted to give you your schedule. Huỳnh here can show you to your first class."

I look between them. "That won't make her late?"

Huỳnh smiles. "Remember, Avery, time isn't real."

"Right," I say, scrunching my eyebrows. I wonder what exactly the extent of that is. How does it work? And why do we have the night off if time doesn't exist? Why are there schedules?

"Kidding," Huỳnh says after watching my mind's gears grind to a stiff halt. "We're just up early. It won't be a problem." She takes my paper schedule, which is a heavy parchment and smooth as silk.

After she hands it back, I scroll through the classes. History of Heaven and Earth. Enochian. Fencing. General Martial Arts. Demonic Symbols. Intro to Flying.

I'm so enraptured by "Intro to Flying" that I have to go back over the schedule. When my mind catches up with me, the next to last course finally absorbs into my brain.

Demonic Symbols.

"What is this class for?" I ask, my throat tightening. My lungs suddenly don't work. Why would we need to know anything about demons in Heaven? The answer lingers in the depths of my mind, but I can't be the one to say it.

Huỳnh glances at where I'm pointing. She tilts her head, and her eyebrows are upturned. "Demonic Symbols? It's mostly summoning spells and exorcism rituals. You won't need to get into the really intense stuff until your second term."

Summoning? Exorcising?

I force the breath out of my lungs slowly. "Huỳnh," I say slowly, "Why exactly is there a school in Heaven?"

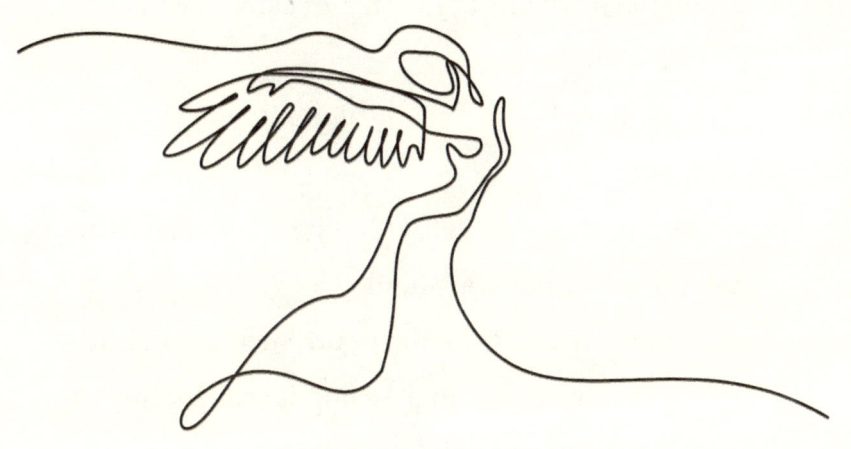

Chapter Six

Huỳnh's mouth pops open at the question. "Oh no. Nobody told you." She suddenly looks worried, and she wraps her arms around herself. The light from her pearlescent wings dims just a little.

"Told me what?" I breathe. I fear that I don't actually want to know the answer to that question, but I know I'm going to get it.

She looks around, then rests a hand on my shoulder. "Avery, Theaa Academy is where angels are trained to kill demons."

All the air is sucked out of the room, and my

vision narrows until Huỳnh's freckled face is all I can see.

Am I dying?

Again?

"Avery, breathe," Huỳnh says. "I mean, you don't need to, but you should."

I follow her instructions and suck in a shuddering breath. Then, after letting it out, another. It brings no relief, though.

"Focus on the timing. Five seconds in, five seconds out."

I do the count, then again, then again. When I'm finally calm enough to gather my thoughts, I come to the realization that we're standing in the center of a hallway, and several students —some with wings, some without—have to dodge around us.

Huỳnh pulls me to the side and sits me on a bench. I let her maneuver me, as there's not much I can do for myself right now. I stare at the floor, focusing on her shoes. They're old-fashioned, a pair of high-heeled shoes with pointed toes.

"Cute shoes," I breathe, my words strained.

"Avery," she says, rubbing a hand on my back,

"you weren't supposed to find this out today. Did you get a letter last night?"

I shake my head, then pause. "I don't know. I fell asleep pretty quick."

When I look up at her, she's nodding. "That explains it. You're supposed to get a detailed explanation your first night, but you must have missed it."

She takes my hand in hers. "It's gonna be okay," she says. "It's not so bad, and there are so many more ups to Heaven than that one negative. And, if you think about it, we're protecting both Heaven and Earth by doing this. It's kind of amazing."

I nod, but it's hard for me to see what's good about this. I'm going to encounter demons? I'll have to fight? Demons?

"I don't know if I can do this," I say honestly. I've never had my own responsibilities, and I've never been much of a fighter, unless you count the one time I punched a guy in the face for harassing my friend. My...teammate? The word isn't quite right. The face of the person I was defending doesn't follow the rest of the memory. When I try to latch onto it, it slips away. Oh, well. It must not matter that much.

"Hey," another voice says. How long has Gabe been standing there? "It's gonna be fine. We were just as freaked out as you when we showed up. You're gonna be alright."

I shut my eyes tight and nod. After a few more seconds of Huỳnh's breathing exercise, I open them.

"Okay," I say. "But I need to get something out of my room."

Before they can ask anything, I stand up, smiling unsteadily. As soon as I turn the corner, I run.

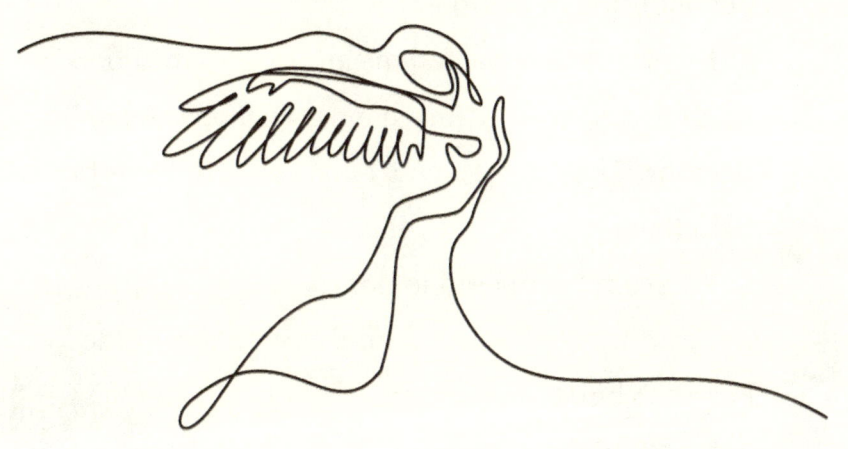

Chapter Seven

I run back the way we came, to the mess hall doors and the spiral staircase. I spot another doorway across the hall, and I sprint through it. There, I end up back in the hospital ward. There's nothing on the other side, but I check the windows. There's got to be a staircase or something down the mountain, right? Or maybe a way to get to God? The Creator? Whatever? I have to let someone know that they've made a big mistake. I'm absolutely not demon-fighting material.

I spin around and go back, all the way through the mess and up the spiral staircase. Maybe I can get out through my room?

I slam the door behind me and sink to the floor, holding my head in my hands. Demons. Actual demons. They're real, and I am going to have to fight them.

What am I supposed to do?

I grit my teeth to keep all this emotion inside, but a sob bursts out anyway.

I can't do this.

I absolutely cannot do this.

After a while, I rest my head against the door. I should have tears streaming down my cheeks, but my eyes aren't even foggy.

A soft knock sounds at my door.

"Avery, come on," Gabe says. "We've gotta get to class."

I grit my teeth and stare at the clouds going past my window. The sky is golden just like yesterday, and I can just see a crescent moon and stars in the lavender distance.

I sigh.

I have to do this. If I'm not cut out for this, why would I have been put here? There must be a reason I got into Heaven and she—whoever she was—didn't.

I stand and open the door.

Gabe and Huỳnh are standing there, and their eyes are filled with concern.

"It's gonna be okay," Huỳnh says softly. "I promise."

I nod, but my jaw is still tight.

Gabe looks away from my eyes after a moment. "We should probably get going. Class is starting soon."

I sigh and step out, closing my door behind me.

"Let's do this."

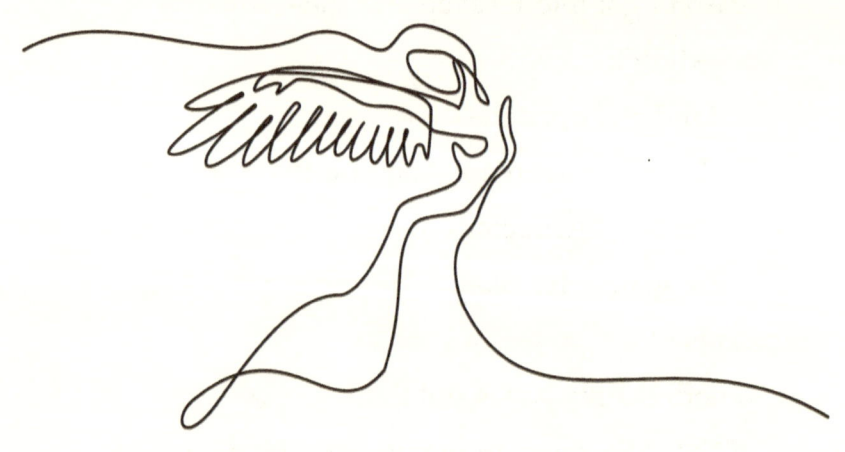

Chapter Eight

As it turns out, Theaa Academy classes are no more exciting than those at Brookstown High School, despite the golden filigree and marble walls. It may look fancier, but, in the end, it's still a class full of teenagers. Sort of.

My mind swirls with confusing symbols from both my Enochian and Demonic Symbols classes, and Intro to Flying is all anatomy and lecture. Not nearly as exciting as expected.

At least fencing, my first class of the day, wasn't too bad. We hadn't been given weapons, but we were given uniforms and taught stances. It's better than a normal gym class, and my new life as an angelic protector means that I apparently don't get worn out. Martial Arts is much the same, and I hope that I don't get the stances mixed up when we do them all over again.

Gabe and Huỳnh aren't in any of my classes, but I am partnered with Nicolai, a blonde boy with a serious face and tousled ice-white hair in Fencing. He seems nice enough, if a little quiet.

"Cause of death?" I say on day two in an attempt to make casual conversation.

He seems surprised for a moment, then smirks. "Drowing."

I grimace. "Sounds miserable. Car went off a cliff," I say.

"Impressive," he says, moving into the second position at Gabriel's instruction. I'd expected a muscular man in flowing white robes with long blonde hair, but instead, Gabriel is short and narrow, every part of him dark, from his fencing uniform to his skin to his eyes. Even his hair is a darker shade of brown, the darkest I've seen besides Azrael.

"Avery, shoulders straight," he says in passing.

When I get out of my final class on day two, Huỳnh is waiting for me in the mess.

"How do you like it now?" she asks, patting the seat next to her.

I sit down and haul a giant book onto the table. "I already have homework in Demonic Symbols. Nobody told me that Heaven included home-work."

She laughs. "Tell me about it. I haven't had homework in decades, but now I have two essays due in as many weeks."

I nod. "Must be rough."

She shrugs noncommittally. "We were called to a higher purpose. I try to honor that by doing my best."

Did I make friends with the most devout person in the world? Or is she just trying to keep me on the right track?

I sigh and open my book, and she helps me in-terpret some of the more complex symbols. I have to copy down a sentence in the Demonic language, and then translate it into English.

"I have a question," I say, pulling my head out of the homework for a short break.

Huỳnh looks up from her own assignment, an essay about Hellish Politics. Terrifying to think about, yet somehow still boring in practice.

"How is it that everyone in Heaven speaks English?"

She tilts her head. "They don't. In fact, I think you're the only American I'm friends with. I was born and raised in Vietnam." She points across the table at Gabe, who has earbuds in while he works on his Creator and Angel Relations assignment. "He's from Puerto Rico."

"So it's like Heaven is a giant TARDIS?" I ask excitedly.

Huỳnh's eyebrows bunch together. "That word doesn't translate."

I roll my eyes. "It's from Doctor Who. The TV show."

"Ah," she says slowly. "I'm more of a book person."

I think of the copy of Jane Austen's Greed and Gentility on my nightstand, which I still haven't started. Too bad there's not a movie. I'm more of a modern romance type of person, although apparently that definition is pretty fluid in Heaven, a place where time isn't real.

"If I'm reading your book, you'll have to watch my show. We could make a night of it tonight." I pause, then add, "But you're not allowed to skip the ninth Doctor. A bunch of people do, but it's basically sacrosanct."

She considers it for a moment, then sighs melodramatically. "Fine. Then you'll have to tell me how you feel about the first five chapters of the book before we start it."

I groan. "Fine." It'll be worth it if I can get another Whovian in the dorms.

This place may be a tiny bit terrifying, but at least I'm starting to get the hang of it.

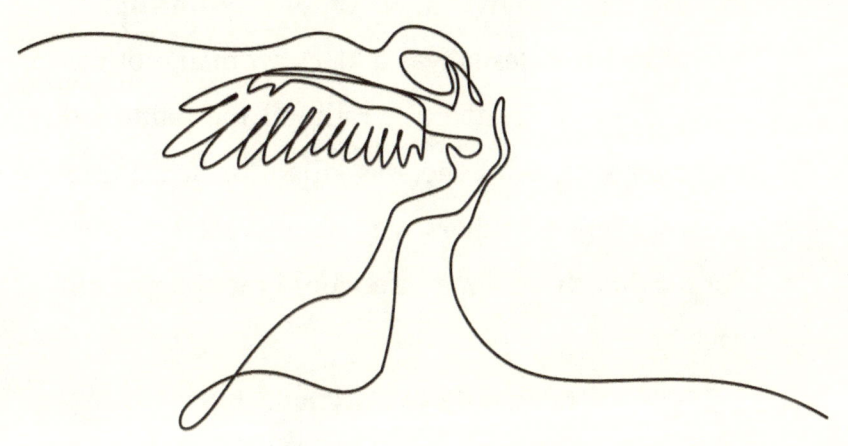

Chapter Nine

O ver the weekend, because at least there are weekends in Heaven, we finish the first season of the modern Doctor Who, and I manage to make it halfway through the Austen novel. If I didn't, Huỳnh would probably stop speaking to me. At least I get to choose the next book when we're done with it. At this point, book club includes a few students from my first term classes, which means I'm not the only one without wings.

I'm getting better at my physical classes, but the theory is just not sticking. As it turns out, the Bible got a lot of stuff wrong, so my limited Christian experience is pretty much completely unhelpful. As it turns out, Jesus was a black woman, not the white man depicted in literally all the paintings I've ever seen. And she was killed for beheading several Roman soldiers who abused their power, not for preaching. That info would piss people off back home.

I spend the evenings doing book club, watching movies, and studying. I still sleep every night, but only for a few hours. As it turns out, I'm not quite sure what to do with nearly unlimited free time. I glance at Huỳnh's wings with envy. If I had some of those, maybe I could fly around.

I'm sitting in my room in the middle of a weekend afternoon, watching a reality TV show that I was obsessed with on Earth, when a loud BOOM shakes the ground. I stand up, stumbling toward the door. When I open it, several other heads are poking out into the hallway.

"What was that?" I ask Huỳnh across the hall.

She shrugs, looking unperturbed, but then it happens again. A boom that tosses us to the side just enough to be concerning.

"Please tell me there are Earthquakes here. Heaven-quakes, I mean." I grip my doorway like it's a lifeline. Unfortunately, Huỳnh shakes her head.

I'm the first to step out of my room, and I stumble down the spiral staircase. Maybe someone in the mess hall or around the classrooms can enlighten me.

But there's nobody around. I trace my steps back and end up in the hospital wing. There's never anybody here, and I wonder if it might just be a welcome area to transition new students into Theaa.

When I step through the doorway, something is wrong. The marble doesn't shine like it did before, and the beds are askew. One shining silver table is tipped on its side.

"Hello?" I call, but there is no answer. Where are all the teachers? Just as I'm about to turn around, a dark figure with shining white wings darts past the window. I sigh with relief. That must be Gabriel. He can tell me what's happening.

I stroll over, but he doesn't notice me. He hovers

45

in mid air, sunlight filtering through his feathers to somehow make him even more angelic.

I open the window. "What's going on?" I call.

He darts his eyes to me, and they widen. "Go back to your room. Tell all the students to lock their—" he's cut off by a writhing black figure crashing into him, all limbs and claws and smoke. I can't focus on it, not because it's moving too fast, but because every time I try, my vision blurs.

What the hell is that thing?

I turn to run when the glass windows behind me shatter all at once. I fall to the floor, breathless. Something heavy skitters over the glass, then lands directly in the center of my back. Talons dig into my shoulders, and I try to reach around to remove whatever it is, but I can't seem to get a grip on it.

I cry out when one of the talons penetrates my skin. Is that something that can happen in heaven? Can I actually be hurt? Molten gold drips out from my shoulder, and I gasp at the sight. The wrongness of it stops my writhing. Something clatters to the ground in front of me, and I lift my head as high as I can with the creature breathing down my neck and tearing at my skin.

A sword.

I reach out, my fingers barely brushing it. The thing attacking me tightens its hold, and I let out a shriek as a sharp pain slices down my back just as I my hand grasps the sword. Electricity races up my arm, and a rightness settles in my gut.

Tears prick at my eyes, and I plunge the heavy sword blindly behind me. The creature screeches, the sound absolutely deafening right next to my ear. Its claws release from my flesh, and black goop spills out over me, hissing and bubbling but not doing any harm to my body. I close my eyes as the liquid runs over my face.

After a mere moment, the weight disappates from my completely. Like it was never there. Even the disgusting goo sticking to my skin fades.

"Avery, are you alright?" Gabriel asks, but I can't bring myself to turn and look at him.

I open my mouth to speak, but the words won't come out.

Am I alright? What the hell was that thing?

"Avery, I need you to sit up," another voice says.

Azrael. She helps me, her hands gentle. Why can't I see her though? I cover my face with my empty hand, but the bright white in front of my eyes doesn't go away.

"I think she was bitten," Gabriel says.

Bitten? What the hell?

"Avery, you're going to be alright. We will treat your injuries, and you will be fine in a few hours. But I need you to close your wings so we can carry you," she says.

Wings?

Her words don't make sense. It can't be possible. Aren't I supposed to undergo some sort of vague ceremony at the end of term to get my wings?

I close my eyes—they're useless right now anyway—and focus on all the muscles in my body. The problem is, there are several new ones, which are sprouting from the center of my back, right where that burning agony had been moments ago.

"I can try," I croak. When did my throat get so dry?

There's a shuffling of feathers against each other, but it's hard to tell exactly what I'm doing when

I can't see these clumsy new appendages.

"It's alright," Gabriel says, his voice eternally calm. "Take your time."

Finally, they're tight against my back, and the archangels help me to a standing position. I lean on Azrael, who tells me where to step as we go. I want to reach behind me and feel the wings, but one hand is far too heavy, and the other is wrapped around Azrael's shoulder.

"We're going back to your room," she says. "You'll be more comfortable there."

I am so glad I can't see the stares that must be focused on me when we reach the housing wing. There are mumbles as I come through, though. Some are shocked, and some are disapproving. I try my best to block out the words.

"Are you okay?" Huỳnh asks, another hand landing on my shoulder. "How did this happen?"

Azrael's voice is filled with dread.

"Demons were able to infiltrate Theaa Academy. We were able to fend them off, though." She pauses to whisper my room number. "Avery killed one."

The mumbles of the other students turn to whispers, and I can't help but strain to hear their now hushed words. What are they saying about me?

More importantly, how did I manage to kill a demon and sprout wings after only just arriving here?

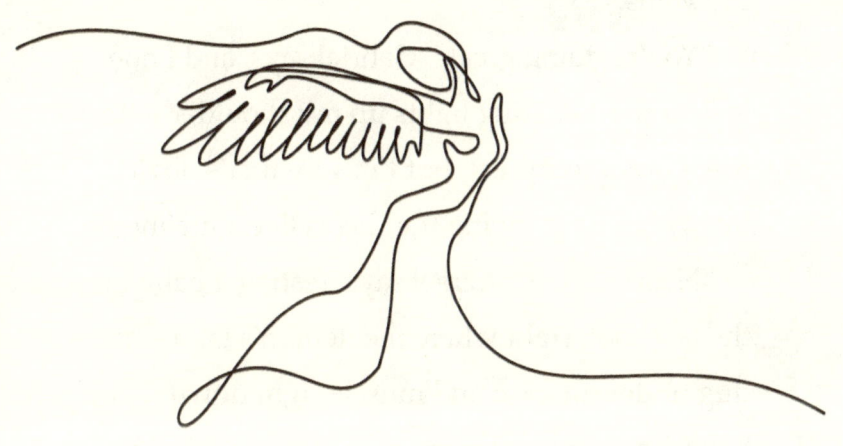

Chapter Ten

O nce I'm seated in my bed, Gabriel says, "Avery, we need you to let go of the sword."

Until now, I hadn't even realized that I still have the sword tight in my grip, the leather of the handle practically embedded into my palm. I lift each finger individually, and the weapon clatters to the floor. When it's gone, I let out a sigh of relief. That's why my arm had been so heavy.

Azrael begins to clean my wounds, and, despite her care, it still hurts like hell. I gasp and grip the sheets. At least I don't have to look at the apparently golden blood that's flowing through my veins.

"You're doing great," Gabriel says, and I nod just as another sting lights up my shoulder with fire. I don't feel great, but I'm sure that's obvious by my hands gripping the sheets like a lifeline.

"Nearly done," Azrael says, resting a palm on the last spot, right where the demon's talons had dug under the skin and muscle right down to the bone. I cry out as she scorches my skin, clenching my hands tight so I don't move. My nails bite into my palms.

"How did demons even get in?" I ask to distract myself. "This is Heaven. Actual Heaven." As if I need to clarify.

Azrael sighs and releases my shoulder, but the burn is still there. At least it's beginning to ebb. "Honestly, we aren't sure. It's happened before, but it's been…A while."

I nod, although I'm not quite sure I understand. The fact that they don't know what happened is making me uneasy. If they don't know how it happened, then they don't know how to prevent it from happening again. My stomach rolls, something so unexpected that it gives me pause. Do angels vomit?

The new muscles that attach at my shoulder blades tense.

Angels.

I'm an angel. A freaking angel. I thought that being friends with angels would make this a simple transition, but I guess it never really absorbed that I would become one, too.

"I think I need to sleep," I say. My vision has slowly begun to come back, fading from total whiteness to vague blurry shapes. "It's been a lot."

After a pause, Gabriel says, "Alright. Take all the time you need."

When the door closes behind them, I lie on my stomach. My wings are huge and awkward, and I don't think I can figure out how to be comfortable on my back or side with these things taking up so much space.

Maybe I should've paid more attention in Intro to Flying. I can't even picture the anatomy of my wings to move them properly.

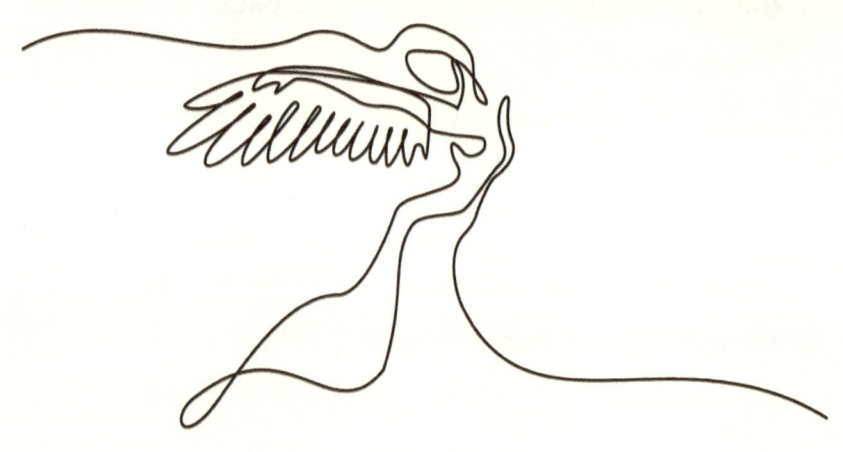

Chapter Eleven

When I awaken, eyesight back to normal, there's a letter on my desk, along with a package. I pick up the brown box that's tied with a pearl white ribbon, but I read the letter first.

Please report to classes as usual. The package enclosed should help with your wings. -G.

My mouth twists into a frown, but I open the package anyway. The leather straps enclosed cause me to burst into a fit of giggles.

It's a harness. Of course.

As it turns out, wrestling unfamiliar fourteen-foot wings into a harness on one's back is not a simple task. When I'm done, though, my wings tuck neatly against my pristine uniform, and I'm grateful that I won't be able to accidentally hit anybody with them. They're huge, and, although I haven't tested them out, the muscles feel tightly wound and ready to spring into powerful action. I could really do some damage with these things if I wanted to.

I take the door handle, but I hesitate. The sword is lying on my desk, and I'm not sure what I'm supposed to do with it. It's blinding silver with pearl white leather wrapped around the hilt, and Enochian runes are embedded all the way up the blade. I look at the door, then the sword.

Maybe it's Gabriel's, and I'm supposed to re-turn it? I sigh and grab it off the desk, shoving the blade through one of the harness straps, as I don't have any sort of sheath to keep it in. This will do for now. It's not like I can keep a magical sword in my room anyway. Wouldn't that be a rule violation about weapons? It's hard to tell, as I never got a student handbook.

If I don't go now, I'll be late, so I step into the

hallway. A few students are still milling around, and they all pause to stare at me. Most of them are wingless, and the one girl who has wings isn't wearing a harness. I set my jaw. If I'm going to get stares for how ridiculous I look today, then I will have to own it.

This will be fine.

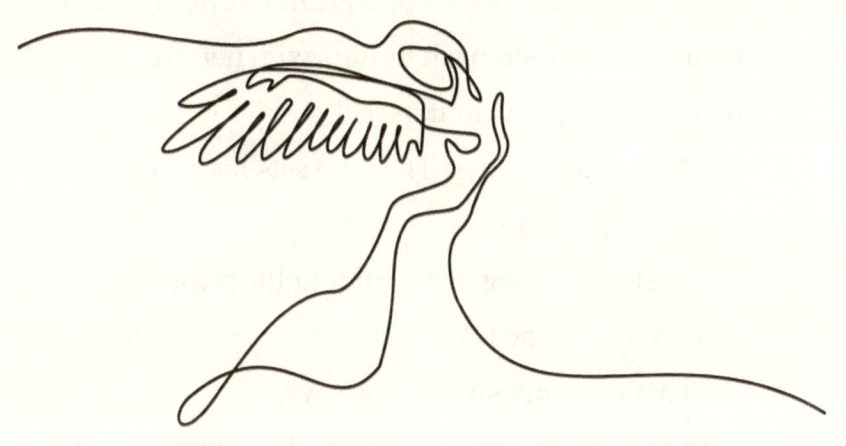

Chapter Twelve

The only way to manage my day is for me to stride into class like I own the place. Fencing is the very first class I have, so I march up to the front of the class and pull the sword out, turning the handle to Gabriel.

He just raises his eyebrows at me. "What is this?" he asks.

I am viscerally aware of everyone's eyes on me. This is a beginner-level class, and I have freaking wings strapped to my back, itching to escape and spread out.

"The sword I used to kill the demon yesterday,"

I say. My voice may be powerful, but my heart is racing, and my stomach flutters with nerves. "I figured you might want it back."

"Ah," is all he says. Then, he sets his pen down and crosses his arms.

I'm still standing here, holding the sword out to him. Why isn't he taking it?

"That's not my sword," he says.

Every pair of eyes is on us right now. Oh, god. What do I do?

He smiles, although he doesn't show teeth, and his eyes are tight. "That's your sword," he says.

But that doesn't make any sense.

He continues, "When the demon hurt you, you were able to summon your weapon. Some get scythes, others get axes, some shields. You were given a sword."

Oh. My eyes widen as I think of the implications. I was given a sword? How is that decided? Who decides that?

"Avery, you are an angel now, but your training is nowhere near where it would normally be when you go through this change." He drops his arms and takes the sword in one hand. He swipes it side to side, then balances it by the guard. "It's a lovely weapon. It will work well." He sets it on his desk. "But for now, I'd prefer if you used the foils like the rest of the class. You can pick this up before you go back to your dormitory at the end of the day."

I nod, relief flooding me. At the very least, I won't have a sword sticking out of my belt all day. I've got enough for people to ogle at as-is.

"Is it true you killed a demon?" Nicolai asks, raising his foil to me, and I match his stance.

I nod. "I mean, it was that or die." I pause. "Can angels die? I mean, we're dead already."

He shrugs. "I wouldn't know. Haven't gotten to that part in class." He lunges at me, and I block him. He uses the moment to whip his sword around and tap me on my waist. I groan. "For a full-fledged angel, you kind of suck," he laughs.

I roll my eyes, and we go back to our starting stances.

The rest of my day is filled with every variety of interaction possible, from Nicolai's lighthearted humor to the endless badgering of students in my other classes.

Finally, when we're let go from Intro to Flying, a humiliating lesson where the teacher stretched one of my wings out to demonstrate the different muscles and their functions, I go back to Gabriel's classroom.

"Here," he says, passing my sword back to me. Now, though, it's encased in a sheath, which shines and glistens like a transparent opal. I can just make out the sigils that are engraved down the blade. I should definitely study harder, because I can only figure out a couple of them.

Before I make it back to my room, Huỳnh catches up with me. "How's it feel?" She asks, clapping a hand on my shoulder. She's sporting an excited grin.

I tilt my head. "How does what feel?"

She laughs. "Being an angel. Pretty amazing, right?"

I frown. "I don't know. My wings hurt." There's a sentence I never thought I'd say.

She glances at my back. "That's because you've

got this thing on." She snaps one of the harness straps against my skin—no, my feathers—then looks around. "Put your sword away and come with me."

What is she up to? I hide the sword under my bed like I used to do with contraband romance novels back home, then meet her back in the hall. She takes my hand and leads me downstairs, then across the school until we're outside. Outside. I spread my arms and take in a deep breath. A lot of the walkways are mostly open to the air, but they're still enclosed in some way. This is the first time I've been outside since coming here.

"Ready?" Huỳnh asks. Before I can reply, she unclips my harness, and my wings spring free. They stretch out, and I have to close my eyes to figure out which muscles do what. Who knew that having brand-new muscles could be so complicated? I groan at the feeling of relief that this brings. Being out of the harness feels absolutely incredible, and a cool breeze flows around us, ruffling through my sensitive feathers.

I have feathers. I open my eyes and grin at

Huỳnh.

"Ready to fly?" she asks.

My eyes widen.

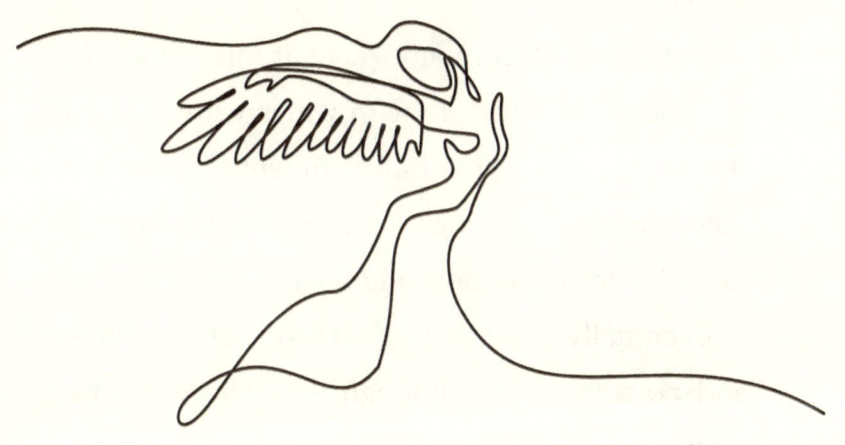

Chapter Thirteen

Unsurprisingly, flying for the first time ever is a lot more difficult than it seems. I can't even get myself off the ground, as my wings just won't cooperate. Eventually, I give up and sit on the ground, watching Huỳnh rise and plummet above me. Another student joins her. Is that Gabe? I squint, but I can't be sure.

My face falls, but I try to stay positive. At least I'll be ahead of the rest of my class when they do get their wings. I focus on my muscles, flexing and releasing. If I can just get used to the way they feel, maybe I'll be able to figure out the flying part.

I sigh.

I really don't fit in anywhere at this school. To my peers, I'm a weirdo with wings who can't do the basics, and to the older students who've already gotten their wings, I'm just an inexperienced girl who doesn't understand them.

Eventually, I wave halfheartedly at Huỳnh—and possibly Gabe, although they haven't come close enough for me to tell—and go back to my room after strapping my wings back in. I'm still not confident that they'll stay against my back for long if I leave them out. Any unconscious movement is multiplied tenfold by their sheer size. Why do wings have to be such huge, physical things? Aren't we supposed to be ethereal beings? Wings made of light would be way easier to handle.

When I go in my room, it's a little cramped. Now I understand why Huỳnh's room is so spacious. Otherwise, there wouldn't be room for her wings. Just as I'm thinking that, the space stretches out, and the ceiling moves upward.

Well, at least renovating is an easy process.

I sigh and sit at my desk. I could spend the night

feeling sorry for myself, or I could buckle down and get my homework done. I opt for the second. The distraction will be good for me.

I do the reading for History of Heaven and Earth, and something in the writing catches my attention.

There are several qualifying factors to be accepted into Heaven, but the most important is behaving with empathy. One must put others before themselves if they are to be accepted into Heaven. This can be seen with historical examples such as Mother Theresa, Nicola Tesla, and Jeanne de Clisson.

I think back to my unnaturally short life. I wasn't that old when I died, but I certainly didn't live with empathy. Every single thing I did was for survival. I didn't have time for empathy. After Mom died, Dad stopped caring. If I couldn't take care of myself, I wouldn't have made it.

A niggling voice in my head reminds me that I did not, in fact, make it.

My heart sinks as I read on. Although Jeanne de Clisson was a murderous pirate, she saved a lot of people by destroying a large number of the French ruling class.

Maybe the fact that I didn't kill anybody counted toward me?

Seems unlikely, though. The only person I cared about in the end was...

The name doesn't come to me. I can think of every other person in my life, but not her. I wrack my brain for the information, but it's like it's been sliced out with a surgical scalpel.

Why can't I figure this out? Why is she gone?

My breathing quickens, and I stare at the page for far too long.

What does this mean?

Am I even supposed to be here? Or has there been a horrible mistake?

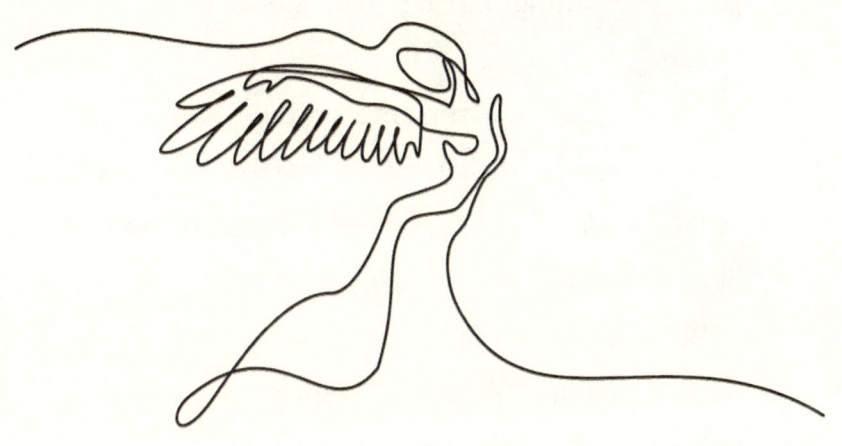

Chapter Fourteen

I pay attention in class. I do all my homework. I offer to help clean up at the end of Fencing, and I try harder to participate in Huỳnh's book club. I even pick a book the others might enjoy. Twilight should be simple enough, right? Romance seems to be a theme with this group.

Still, I can't shake the niggling feeling that something is wrong with me. No matter how much I try, I can't remember the girl from the meadow, the girl who'd been in the car with me when I died. Why did I make it into Heaven, and she didn't? There's something I'm missing, a puzzle piece that will explain everything, but it's just...gone. Like it was stolen.

"Good job," my sparring partner, Jenine, says after a particularly strenuous martial arts lesson. We're working on Taekwondo, and I'm getting okay at it.

"Thanks," I say, shaking her hand. Does she see something I don't? Does my being here make sense to her? I consider asking, but what if there was a mistake and I'm not supposed to be here? Would asking about it arouse suspicion? I've been treated with nothing but kindness since I arrived, but if I slip up, that could change in an instant.

"Avery, may I speak with you?" Azrael says as I'm leaving class. I swallow and do my best to quell my ever-rising panic.

"Sure," I say as casually as I can.

I enter her classroom as everyone else is heading out to their afternoon activities. I was supposed to work on a Demonic Symbols assignment with Nicolai, but I'm sure he'll understand. Or he won't, and I'll be found out. Maybe I should have told Azrael that I'm supposed to be somewhere.

But that might make it look like I'm avoiding her. There's no good answer here.

"Take a seat," she says. Her face appears open and relaxed, but how can I be sure? "Would you like some hot chocolate?"

I'm about to say no, but I don't want to seem panicked. "That would be great!" I say with far too much enthusiasm.

She waves her hand, and a cup of steaming cocoa appears. I wonder if there will be marshmallows, and they appear in the cup. I take it, and the warmth grounds me in this moment. I just have to think positive.

"How are you adjusting?" she asks, folding her hands together and resting her chin on them. Her dark hair is pulled into a French twist, but one curl escapes just ahead of her ear.

I shrug. "Okay. I'm in a book club."

She smiles. "That's fantastic. I know that some students have trouble making friends when they first arrive, but it seems that you've been taken in by a few others." She pauses, then puts her hands down on the table. "I did want to ask, though, how you're feeling about everything else." She gestures at me, I assume at my wings.

I shrug once again. Am I shrugging too much? How often do people normally shrug? "Not bad, I think. I get a lot of attention, but there's not much I can do about that."

She nods, then purses her lips. "I was thinking," she says slowly, "that we might move you up to a few of the term two classes.

Every muscle in my body tenses. "I don't know." My words are short and betray my anxiety. Surely being surrounded by upper-class students would make it clear that there's something wrong with my being here.

She rests a hand over mine, and her face is still nothing but kind. "That's alright," she says. "Although I do think you need something to make up for your...extra abilities."

I laugh a short, nervous laugh. "You mean extra appendages?"

She smiles back, humor in her eyes. At least she seems to be mistaking my anxiety for nerves about working with the advanced students. "Exactly. I

think you could benefit from extra swordsman-
ship lessons with Gabriel, and I could help you to
control your wings. I've seen you practicing with
your friends, but, in this case, I think a more experienced hand would do you some good."

I take a sip of my drink, and it warms me from
the inside out. So that's what this is all about. She's
not suspicious of me whatsoever. Maybe I'm just
overreacting. "That sounds better," I say slowly. "I
don't want to be more out of place than I already
feel." I shouldn't have said that last part, but she
doesn't pick up on my extra reasons for feeling
wrong.

She nods, considering. "Alright, I'd like you to
meet with me over the weekend. You don't have to
wear your uniform.

I nod, then stand to go, setting the mostly-full
hot chocolate back on her desk. "Thanks," I say.
"Now, if you'll excuse me, I'm supposed to be
helping Nicolai with a project."

She waves me off, and I have to try to not sprint
out of her office.

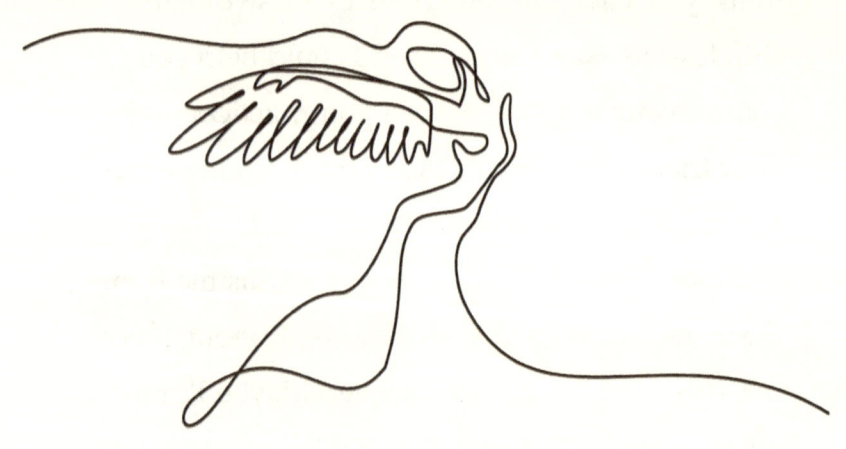

Chapter Fifteen

"Isn't it interesting how similar Enochian Sigils are to Demonic ones?" Nicolai asks, tossing a chip in his mouth.

I tilt my head. "They are?" I ask, then look back at the papers. Well. He's right. They're nearly identical. How did I not make that connection? "Huh."

He nods. "I saw some of these before I died. There were a lot of old churches in Saratov." He pauses, then clarifies. "Russia."

"Got it," I say, flipping the page in my textbook. "I'm from Oregon. I could basically see you from my house."

He seems confused at the last sentence, and I wave it off. "It's a joke from an American politician from Alaska."

He nods. "Oh. That's funny." But he doesn't laugh. Apparently not that funny. Or he could just be too busy focusing on this horrible assignment. We're supposed to translate an entire passage, although I don't understand why these pages don't translate into English automatically like everything else seems to.

I ask Nicolai about it out loud.

"It's because these aren't human languages," he says. Then, he smiles. "Maybe if you paid attention in class, you would know that."

I roll my eyes. He's always teasing me about things. It's all in good fun, but it makes me feel like I'm not good enough.

I do have wings and a sword, though. I was good enough to kill a demon, at the very least.

"You do know I'm kidding, right?" Nicolai asks. When I look back up at him, he appears to actually be concerned for my feelings.

I smile, although it's not genuine. "I know."

His mouth twists down, like he's thinking about something. "I'll make fewer jokes," he says.

I really don't like confrontation, and this whole conversation is getting dangerously close to the question of why I'm so different from everybody else. "It's really no big deal." Then, I switch gears. "Do you know what this sentence says?" I point at a random sentence just to change the subject, and he translates it for me to write down. "Thanks."

He smiles. "No problem." Thankfully, he doesn't talk about the joke he'd made, and I don't offer him an opportunity to make assumptions about me. The rest of the study session goes by normally.

"Your wings are amazing, by the way," he says as he's packing up his bag to leave my room. "The other students in our term may say things, but they're just jealous."

I look at the ground. This entire evening has been so uncomfortable for me, and I just want to be alone to binge bad reality TV. I might not even sleep tonight.

He steps toward me, and he's giving me a look, his eyes boring into mine. What is he searching for? Secrets?

Before I can figure it out, he shocks me by pressing his lips to mine.

I jolt away, tripping onto my bed.

"What was that?" I demand, covering my mouth with my hand.

Instantly, his eyes widen. "I'm sorry. I thought…I mean, it seemed like…" His face is turning a deep red, which doesn't make sense considering our blood is apparently liquid gold, but I can't consider the logic too much because he kissed me. What the hell?

I shake my head. "No, Nicolai. It's not like that. I just consider you a friend." I take in a deep breath, putting my hands in my lap and staring at them. So this is why he's been looking at me so much, finding reasons to spend time with me. He's not suspicious at all. "I don't…like boys. Like that."

The silence is deafening. After a moment, he just says, "Oh."

I don't dare look at him.

"That's okay," he finally says when the quiet becomes unbearable. "I like being your friend."

I sigh, the air whooshing out of me along with all the tension.

"I like being your friend, too," I say, and I find that I'm telling the truth. He doesn't ogle at my strangeness, doesn't treat me like a freak, doesn't whisper about me when I pass.

"I'll see you in class tomorrow, he says, giving me a small smile and a half wave.

I smile back, and say, "Yeah. See you."

With that, he's gone, and I bury my face in my pillows. What is happening?

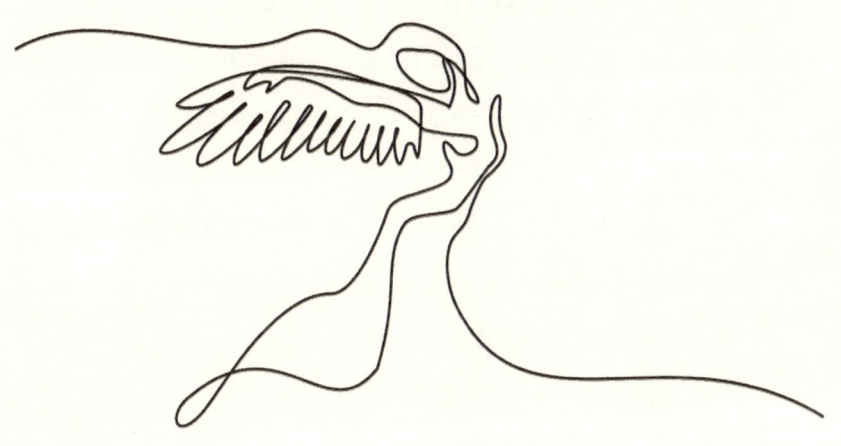

Chapter Sixteen

While we're taking an exam in Enochian class, another boom like the one a few weeks ago shakes the school. We all look up, and Azrael glancess around.

"Stay here," she says, her lips tilting into a frown. And is that fear in her eyes? She leaps out of the window, her wings catching the air instantly.

As soon as she leaves, there are eyes on me. Not everyone in the class is staring, but enough. Nobody says a word.

I could just sit here, waiting and fearing, but I can't stand the thought of being a sitting duck. My sword is still tucked under my bed. Maybe I could do it again. Maybe I could keep us safe.

When I lock eyes with Nicolai, his jaw sets, and his eyebrows are bunched. He's scared. After a quick glance around, it's clear that they all are. Everyone knows that I nearly died—or double died—when I killed the first demon. If one got in here, would we all survive?

I stand from my desk and grab my bag, running across the school to get to my room. There are no angels in sight, just like last time. Everyone capable of fighting demons must have taken to the sky.

I make it to my room without being attacked, but every slight breeze and settling of the building and crash of the waterfalls startles me. My heart is practically pounding out of my chest.

I make it to my room and grab my sword. It's heavier than I remember, but that same electric charge runs up my arm when I take it. How had I assumed that this sword belonged to anyone but me?

I unsheathe it, and I try to hold the same position that Gabriel has been drilling into me for weeks.

The plan is to go back to the classroom, ready to defend my peers if a demon does show up.

When I open my door, though, there is a demon in the hall. At the sound of my door opening, it turns.

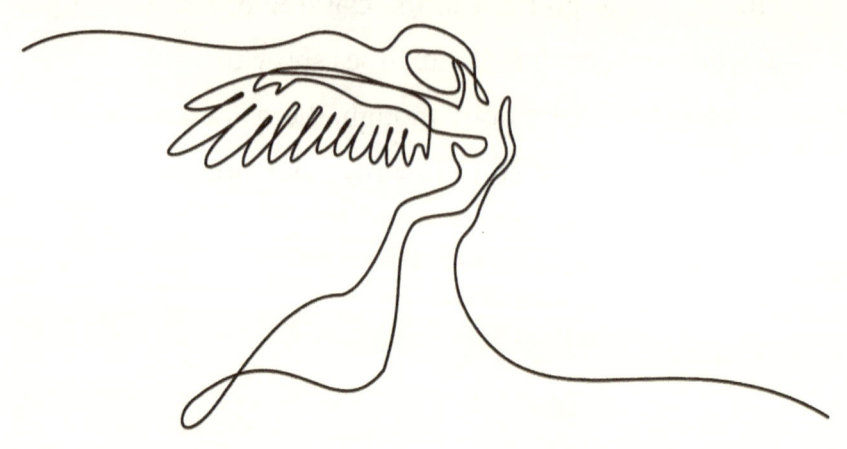

Chapter Seventeen

*D*esireé.

   The name slams into me, and I gasp with pain as my heart tears in two. Every memory that has been repressed, the face that's been hidden from my memories, it all comes back.

   The face in front of me is one I know better than my own. The fact that I've forgotten it at all is inconceivable.

   "Desireé," I breathe, and the creature's eyes widen.

   She looks different. So different. If I didn't know every curve and angle of her body, I wouldn't even know it's her.

Hair that used to be a fiery red is now black as pitch, rolling down her back in waves. Her eyes are almost entirely black as well, seemingly draining the room's light away like a vampire drawing blood from its victim. Her irises, though, are the same icy blue they've always been. Her features are sharper, her cheekbones ready to cut glass. Most notably, she has black spiral horns and dark, leathery wings. She is wrong. Everything about this is wrong, broken.

But it's still her.

"What did they do to you?" I ask, raising a hand. When she lifts hers to me, I flinch. Her hands are black, like they've been dipped in ink, and the tips are no longer human. Instead, she has bird-like talons. My shoulder is long healed, but I can feel those talons under my skin like it was yesterday.

She frowns, her lips a gruesome splash of red against her snow-white skin. If it weren't Desireé, I would think her a monster. But those freckles, which stand out like dried bloodstains on her now impossibly light skin, are as familiar to me as my own heart. I drop my sword.

She darts forward, her hands wrapping around my wrists. She presses me to my door, her strength surprising for her emaciated frame.

Had this all been a trick? Am I going to die?

Her face comes right up to mine, fangs taking up half her mouth and breath made of smoke and fire. Instead of tearing my throat out, though, she presses her lips to mine.

I lean into her, relief flooding my system. "It's you," I say, my voice incredulous. "It's really you." I pull my hands up and run them through her hair. I'm trembling, and I can't help but hold her close as her kisses trail down my cheekbone and then down my neck.

"Avery," she whispers, her voice smoky and dark. My name on her tongue feels like home, and I groan, tightening my hands in her hair.

Far too soon, she pulls away.

"I had to find you," she says. "I've been looking for a way in for months."

Months? "I've only been here a few weeks," I say.

She shakes her head. "Time is different in these places. Way different. What feels like weeks to you has been years to me." Her voice is pained on the word 'years.'

I look her over, tracing my thumbs over her face. "Years?"

She looks at the ground and nods.

A sound at the staircase startles me, and I know exactly what this would look like if anybody were to find us. I whisper my room number and drag her inside, kicking my sword and sending it skittering across my bedroom floor before shutting the door.

She looks around in surprise. At least, that's what it seems to be. Her expression is hard to read now. She's so different than she used to be.

"I know this place," she says slowly.

I tilt my head. "Yeah," I say slowly. "It's my room. From…back home. Bigger, but still a lot like mine."

She hesitates, then sinks onto the enormous mattress. A moan is pulled from her lips.

"Desireé," I say, slowly. I don't want to startle

her. Now that it's all come back to me, I can't lose her again. I just can't. "You said you've been…like this…for years. What did you mean?"

She looks at me, then down at herself. She's wearing all black, and it's hard to tell where one piece of clothing ends and another begins. When she speaks, her voice is laced with shame. The tone breaks my heart. "I wasn't always like this."

I nod. "I know. You used to be…" There's really no polite way to say this, so I just spit it out. "Human."

She nods. "I was punished," she says.

I don't know if I can hear this. My entire body is tensed to run, to get away from whatever she has to tell me.

But I have to hear her.

"That's how it is. They punish you. Until you forget your name. Your face. Your life." She turns her head to look out the window. Her shoulders are tense. I want to tell her she's safe here, but how could that be true? She's a demon in a school of demon killers. When she looks back at me, her eyes shine. "But I never forgot you. That's what got me through. How I resisted so long. I kept you."

My throat closes up. She'd been punished —tortured for years—because of me?

"I knew I had to find you. So I lied. Acted like I didn't remember. And they stopped. The pain stopped. But I looked different." She lifts a hand to her head, her finger tracing the ridged horn on her right side. "I wasn't me anymore. Until you said my name, I didn't know it. I didn't have one.

"And then I was enrolled in Daemaac Academy. It's…like here. But not."

I swallow, then take a step toward her. "What do you mean?"

"It's dark. So dark. When I got here, I thought I'd go blind. There's so much light everywhere." Her voice goes soft and hoarse, breaking like she's been hurt. "How do you stand it?"

I wrap my arms around myself. I'm afraid if I try to touch her, she'll shatter. She'll fall into pieces, and I won't be able to put her back together.

She lifts a hand, almost like she's going to touch me from across the room, then drops it when her eyes find the talons at the end.

That's all the encouragement I need. I stride over to her and pull her into my arms. Her horns are rough as she buries her face in my neck, but I won't let go. She could be tearing my heart out of my chest, and I wouldn't be able to let go.

"You're safe now," I say. "It'll be okay."

"How?" she asks. I don't answer, just stroke her hair.

When I look out the window, the older angels are returning to their classrooms.

If I'm not there, they'll come looking for me. They can't find Desireé here. They'll destroy her. If I don't feel like I belong, she sure as hell won't.

"I have to go," I say, pulling away from her. It's like tearing off one of my limbs, and I grimace. She lets out a little cry, but she doesn't try to keep me in her arms. "I'll be back. If I don't go now, though, they'll find you."

She closes her eyes and nods. I press my lips to her forehead. "I'll be back," I whisper. A promise. She has to be here when I return. I don't know what I'll do if she's not. "Please don't leave."

I pick up my sword, but I don't look back before

leaving. If I do, I'll stay.

I close the door behind me and head back to class.

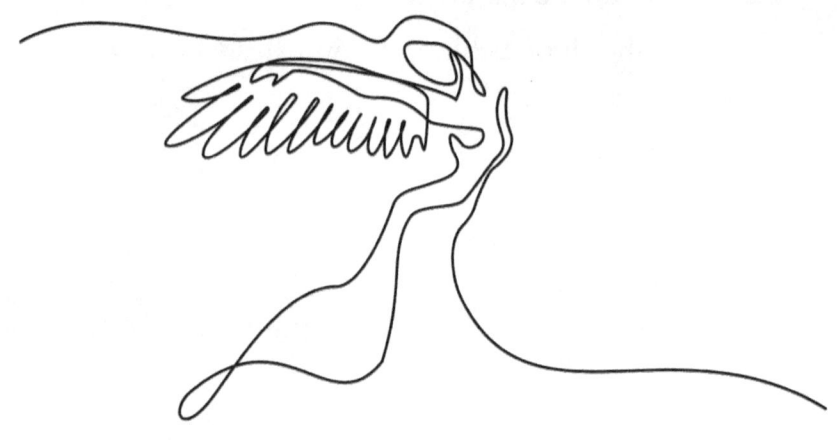

Chapter Eighteen

Everyone stares at me when I return to the classroom. I'm certain I smell like sulfur, but nobody comments. It's almost like they're too intimidated. I recall the disappearance of the original demon that I slayed. If anyone asks, I can just tell them that the same thing happened this time. Nobody has to know.

"Is everyone okay?" I ask, unable to bring forth much energy. I'm exhausted from my racing heart and the revelations of the day.

"Yeah," Nicolai says, his jaw propped open just a little.

I nod and take my seat just as Azrael flies back in, her face grave. "Everyone should go back to their dormitories," she says. Then, she turns to me, a question on her face when she sees the sword. Everyone is already leaving, and she asks me, "Are you alright?"

I nod.

"Did you...?" She doesn't speak the full sentence. I don't want her to, because I'd have to attempt to lie to her. I am so tired of lying to people.

I shrug, casting my eyes downward. Let her make her assumptions. It's better than the truth.

She takes a moment before speaking again. "Would you like to discuss it?"

Instead of answering, I shake my head.

"Will I see you at our lessons this weekend?" she asks. Her voice is filled with nothing but concern for me and my well-being. I almost feel bad in deceiving her.

"Yeah," I say.

No matter how kind she is now, there's no way she would feel the same if she knew what I was hiding in my room.

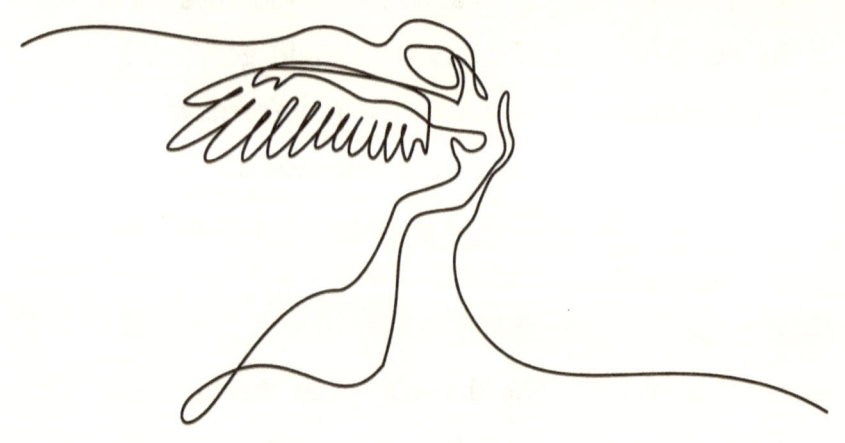

Chapter Nineteen

"What was I like?" Desireé asks that night as I watch her. The longer I look at her, the less terrifying she seems. She may be a demon, but she's also the girl I've known for years, and she's curled up in my giant bed, her head on my pillow. I'm so filled with affection that I could burst.

I scoot my chair forward and take one of her hands in mine. She tried hiding her hands from me when I got back, out of apparent fear that they would make me uncomfortable. Now, though, I stroke the smooth skin and subtle veins below, tracing patterns that only I will remember. I half expect my hands to come away covered in soot, but they're clean.

"You were the kindest person I ever knew," I say. She smiles the tiniest bit, and my heart soars with this small victory. I would die a thousand more times for that smile. "You cared about every single person. And for some reason, you decided that I was your favorite out of all those people."

She sighs, her eyes fluttering shut. I wonder when the last time she laid in a bed was.

"Do you want to sleep?" I ask, lacing my fingers through hers. She's careful to make sure her talons don't dig into the back of my hand.

Her eyes snap back open, and she glances up at me. This close, I can still make out the one tiny gold spot in her otherwise blue irises. It's on her right eye, and her mom used to call it an Angel's kiss. I lean forward and rest my lips on her forehead, a habit I'd forgotten I had until I finally saw her again.

"Sleep?" she asks. Her eyebrows bunch together, and I pull away and smooth out the space between them with the thumb of my spare hand.

"What's that?"

I have to bite my cheek to keep from overreacting and startling her. Exactly how much of herself did she lose down there?

"It's when you close your eyes and lose consciousness. Usually in a comfy bed," I say softly, brushing her loose hair back from her forehead. If she's gone years without sleep, she must be exhausted.

"We weren't allowed to have that," she said. "If we lost consciousness, we were punished."

In this moment, I want nothing more than to destroy the creatures that did this to her. I have to fight to keep my hands from clenching into fists.

"Nobody is gonna hurt you hear," I say. "I promise."

I hope it's not a lie. I will do my best to keep anybody from harming her. For the rest of eternity, it will be my mission to keep her safe.

Her eyes flutter shut once again, and, within seconds, she's asleep, her hand going slack in mine.

Over the next few days, I sneak her food and news. After a close call with Gabe showing up at my door at the end of the week, I picture an enormous walk-in closet instead of my shallow one. It even has a false wall at the back with a plush twin bed on the floor of a cubby. I try to make an entire extra room, but that doesn't seem to be within the bedroom's capabilities. This will have to do.

Saturday, I have my lesson with Azrael in the same field Huỳnh showed me before. I'm getting better at using my wings, although I can still only barely get off the ground.

"You're improving at an incredible rate," Azrael comments when I fall to the ground once again.

I don't feel like it, but I don't tell her that.

By the end of the day, I'm even more frustrated than I was before.

When I get back to my door to spend time with Desireé, Huỳnh takes my arm in hers. I stifle a groan. I just want to be back with Desireé, but avoiding my friends is a good way to get caught.

"How were flying lessons?" she asks, leaning on me. "I haven't seen you much this week."

I shrug. "I'm still terrible at flying. And I've been sleeping a lot this week. People keep staring at me."

The lie comes easily. In fact, ever since Desireé showed up, I haven't slept a wink. I'm too paranoid that someone will walk in while we're both asleep and catch her, although I haven't had so much as a knock at my door since the second demon attack.

"Well, you have to come to book club tonight. We're already halfway through New Moon."

I laugh. Of course they took to that series like fish to water. Or, more accurately, birds to the sky. "I'm not too concerned about missing out. I've read it before. When I was alive."

Huỳnh fakes shock, placing her hand on her chest and gasping. "You picked out a book you've already read? I can't believe you'd betray the book club like this!"

"I know," I say. "I'm a devious one."

Huỳnh laughs as we walk down to the mess hall. I keep my head steadily forward so I'm not tempted to look back at my door, the one Desireé is trapped behind. I so wish I could take her out with me, show her campus, introduce her to my friends. They'd be sure to like her.

I bite my lip. No, Huỳnh and Gabe would slaughter her in a heartbeat if they knew about her.

"Are you okay?" Huỳnh asks, pulling me to a seat. She seems genuinely concerned for me. "You seem really distracted." Then, she lowers her voice. "Is it because of the demon?"

My eyes shoot up to hers, but she merely looks worried. "Demon?" I ask. Stay casual. Stay. Casual.

She nods. "I heard you killed another one when the school was attacked again."

I look away. "Yeah. It's getting to me a bit."

She takes my hand in hers. "Most students have only killed one demon. We go out for occasional patrols after getting our wings, but demons are so rare that the only ones we kill are during our initiation."

This is news to me. I haven't actually learned anything about how angels usually get their wings. "Initiation?"

She tilts her head. "That's how we get our wings.

The same way you got yours. Just not as dangerous. At the end of first term, we have to kill a demon. It's usually subdued, though. Nothing like
what happened to you."

Why am I sick all of a sudden? Aside from Desireé, I should hate all demons. They're the creatures that destroyed her, after all. The creatures
that tried to kill me. The long-healed scars on my
shoulder itch. Still, I can't help but wonder just
how many other demons were good people who
had the humanity tortured out of them. Maybe all
of them.

And if I'd ended up in the same place as Desireé,
there's no doubt the angels would've destroyed
me on sight, too.

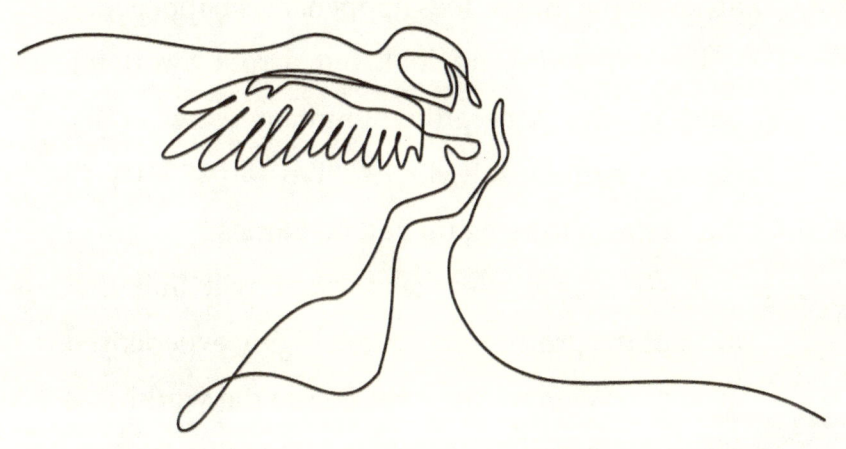

Chapter Twenty

"What happens if an angel is destroyed by a demon?" I ask Azrael after flying practice yields few results.

She studies my face. Instead of answering, she asks, "Are you alright? I've heard you've been sleeping quite a bit since the last attack."

I shrug. "I'm fine. Just curious. I mean, we're already dead, so what could possibly happen afterwards?"

Azrael's eyes bore into mine, studying me for a moment. I refuse to be the first to look away. Eventually, she sighs. "It's been millennia since I've seen an angel die. But it does happen. Has happened."

I bite my lip and look out across the flying field and into where the mountainous waterfalls cascade into the soft clouds. "I'm sorry," I say. "I didn't mean to bring up bad memories."

Azrael shakes her head. "You will find that most of the professors here are highly experienced in battle. We were the first. Before the world was created, there were angels, and there was the Creator."

I nod. I know all this from my History of Heaven and Earth class. We'd covered the pre-history the first two days.

"There was an uprising," she explains. "When the Creator made Earth. An angel and a human."

I don't dare to look at her, but her voice is distant, like she's seeing it all again. This part had been skimmed over, but I know the gist of it.

"Lucifer and Lilith," I say. The angel who fell, and the human woman who refused to serve. I know more about this story from Earth than anything else. When Lucifer fell from the Creator's graces, Lilith had gone with him so she wouldn't have to serve beneath Adam.

I don't tell Azrael how reasonable that seems to me. I'm already desperate to stay as far from the center of attention as I can get. After the recent events that have people staring at me, I just want to hide in my room until they forget.

Azrael sighs. "Yes. With their fall came the creation of Hell. Lilith became the mother of demons, and Adam's child, Cain, became the first murderer, also known by another name."

"What name?" I look back at Azrael, but she's staring off into the clouds like I had been. She doesn't turn to me.

"Death," she says, and my heart thuds solidly in my chest. The word is so much a part of who I am that my reaction shocks me. I thought I'd gotten used to the concept of death by this point, but apparently not. "The name many humans ascribe to me, but I'm much less powerful than Death."

"But wouldn't that make him evil?" I ask. "I mean, he killed his brother. How do we end up here if Cain is…" I struggle with the final word. Death is a concept, right? Not a person. That's just something from movies. If Death is a real person, does that mean the other horses of the apocalypse are real?

Azrael's eyes turn to me. "She was able to atone for her sins. She was granted forgiveness by the Creator, although her eternal penance was to guide the dead to their places in the afterlife."

This information consumes me, but Azrael isn't done talking.

"However, when angels and demons are killed, they are led by Cain to purgatory."

"And what is that?" I ask. I've heard the term, but I know by now that nothing I learned on Earth can be certain.

Azrael cups her palm around my cheek. "That's not something you should have to worry about. No angels have been killed since the original war." The answer frustrates me, but I don't push. Her voice is strained as it is, and I can't bring suspicion upon myself.

"Thanks," I say, smiling just a little to show that I'm satisfied.

She releases me and sucks in a deep breath, then

a peaceful smile spreads across her face. "Go to dinner. Spend time with your friends. I'll see you in class."

I nod and turn to leave.

"And Avery?" she calls just as I'm about to enter the shining castle that I call home.

I stop and glance back.

"Have a good weekend."

I nod and go back to my room.

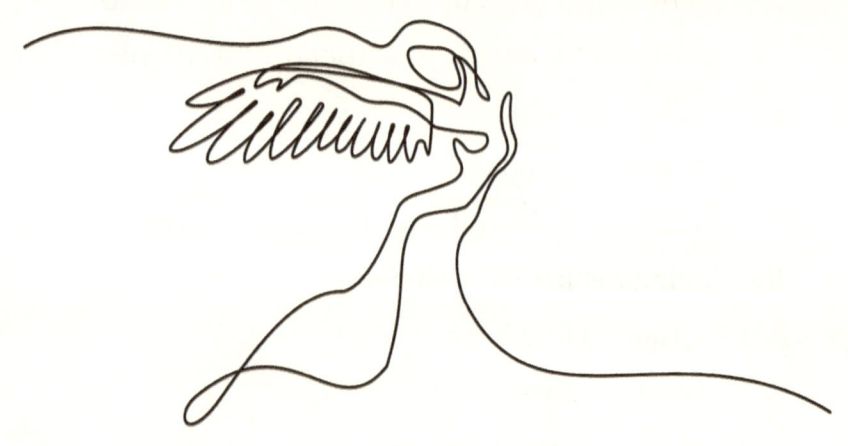

Chapter Twenty-One

Why was I not informed that Theaa Academy had a gigantic library?

I've been standing here gawking at it for so long that Huỳnh grabs my arm. "You alright?" she asks.

I ignore her. There are books. Thousands of books. Probably millions. They're stacked with precision on shelves that tower up to the ceiling, which is stories above us. Each shelf is made of a white stone with glistening gold filigree, and golden letters and numbers are etched into each side.

"Where are the ladders? The stairs?" I breathe.

Huỳnh laughs. "Why would there be any if we

have wings?"

She runs and leaps into the air, catching herself with her wings. I join her, albeit far more clumsily, and my muscles strain at the effort. Now that I'm higher than eye level, though, I realize that the filigree elements double at footholds and handles. There are a couple other students here, some at the ground-level tables, and others using the handles and footholds to scroll through the shelves.

As my wings weaken from exertion, I tilt myself just in time to grab one of the golden handles. I scramble to get my foot on the tiny ledge, my heart racing as I look down.

"I think stairs would help," I say breathlessly to Huỳnh when she joins me. "Or even ladders."

She rolls her eyes and leans back, her weight on the foothold and hand gripped around a single handle. I suppose that she can always catch herself if she falls, but the position makes my heart race.

"What books are you looking for?" she asks, tilting her head back and closing her eyes. I wish I were that confident in my abilities. I'm fairly certain I'm going to have to climb down the shelves to get back to the floor when we're done, and we're not even that far off the ground.

"I'm not really sure. I want to do my History essay on Death and her relationship with Heaven. Where would I even find something like that?" I make the mistake of looking to the ground, and I cling even tighter. *Please don't fall. Please don't fall.*

The midterm essay had been the perfect excuse to learn more about purgatory. If I can find out more about Death, maybe I can figure out why I ended up in Heaven while sweet Desireé landed in Hell. It just doesn't make sense, but maybe I can make sense of it. Is there a way to make an appeal to Death? Or even the Creator? Desireé deserves to be here even more than I do, yet she's trapped in my room, lest she be sent to purgatory or back to Hell. I can't do that to her.

Huỳnh glances around the shelf we're on. "We're in the section about Human History, so…" she squints and stares further up and across. Then, she points. "There. Right at the top. History of Death."

I groan. We're only twenty feet off the ground,

but it feels like a million miles. How am I supposed to make it all the way up there?

Huỳnh evaluates me. "I think you should do it. But I'll show you a trick I learned when I first got my wings."

With that, she turns and hops away, pumping her wings a single time, the powerful muscles propelling her a single level up but on the shelves directly across from us.

"Your turn," she says. Why the hell is she grinning? This is easy for her by now.

I grit my teeth and try the same, but I fumble it so badly that I'm still on the same level, just across from where we were standing.

"Again," Huỳnh says down to me. She demonstrates, and I hop after her. At least this time I end up a little higher. Only one level, but still.

We repeat this process until we make it all the way to the top.

"Don't look down," Huỳnh says as I cling to the side of the shelf, eyes firmly shut.

"Don't worry about it," I gasp. "I'm never opening my eyes again. I live here now. This is my home.

Tell Gabe that we're eating dinner here every day, because I'm not moving."

She laughs, but I don't open my eyes.

"I'm serious," I insist. "If demons want to fight me, they'll have to come up here to do it." My heart is beating out of my chest. I can't believe that I'm hundreds of feet in the air, precariously perched on a library shelf. Can I die from a high fall in Heaven? That shouldn't be possible, right?

"Avery, come on," Huỳnh says. I can practically hear the eye roll in her tone. Of course this is funny to her. When I was alive, though, I couldn't even bring myself to dive off the mid-height diving board at the community pool in the summer.

I open my eyes slowly, keeping my chin tilted up. Is the shelf leaning back? I take in a deep breath. No, it's steady. They probably couldn't fall if we tried.

I stare at the books in front of me, and it takes me a few seconds before I can absorb any of the titles.

"You'll be fine," Huỳnh says. "I promise. If you fall, I'll catch you."

I sigh. "Okay." I don't totally believe her.

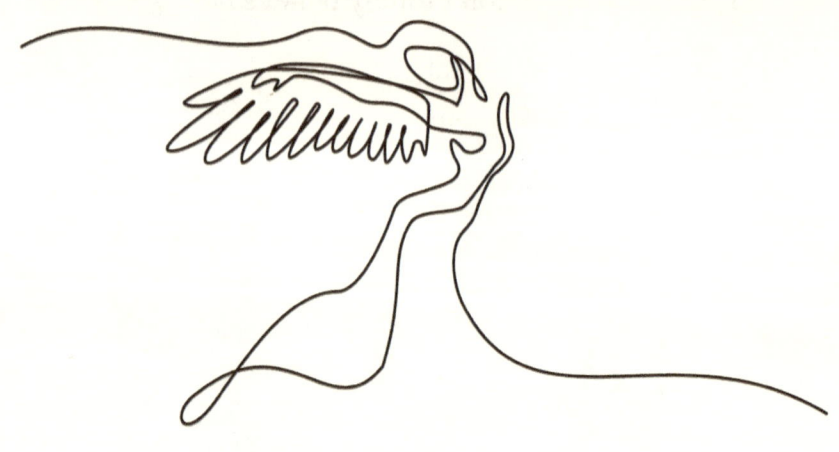

Chapter Twenty-Two

"Can angels get headaches?" I ask, resting my forehead on the chilly desk in my room.

Desireé doesn't reply. I tilt my head to look at her, and she's got a mouthful of ice cream.

"I'm glad you got the room figured out," I say. For the first while, Desireé hadn't been able to convince my room to give her things like food and movies. Now, though, she has a habit of summoning far too many things at once. At least she seems to be getting some of her spark back.

If I can figure this situation out, though, she'll be an angel like me. Things will be back to normal.

Just like old times, but better since we'll have an eternity together.

These old books are all written in Enochian, which means I'm constantly referencing my text-books. So far, I've gotten about half a chapter trans-lated. Good thing I don't actually need to sleep, be-cause I haven't done so in days.

"C'mere," Desireé says, curling a finger at me. She looks both totally creepy and unbearably tempting when she does that.

I stand and stretch, walking slowly toward the bed.

When I get close enough, she dips a claw in her ice cream and smudges it on my cheek.

I squint my eyes and scrunch my nose. "Rude," I say.

Her long tail wraps around my thigh and pulls me even closer, and she licks the ice cream off my cheek.

I suck in a breath, and she puts her hands on my waist, right where my shirt and pajamas meet. Her skin is only touching me by the tiniest sliver, but that spot burns like a thousand suns.

"I have to work on this research," I whisper, but she places her lips against mine.

I moan and lean into the kiss. Maybe I would have more work done if it weren't for moments like this that turn into hours. I tangle one hand in her hair and grip a horn with the other to hold her even closer. Her body pressed against mine lights a fire deep in my belly no matter how many times we kiss.

When she runs her tongue against my bottom lip, I groan and push her into the bed. Her wings spread out behind her while mine are tucked against my body. Within a moment, her leathery wings are wrapped around the both of us, tucking us into a cocoon.

"Avery," she whispers against my hair as I trail kisses down her face and neck. I release her horn and put my hand on her waist, tucking my fingers beneath her shirt. Her claws trail down my eyes back, hard enough to have me gasping, but light enough that it doesn't actually harm me.

I bring my lips back to hers, navigating my tongue into her mouth. I have to be careful to not cut myself on one of her fangs.

A knock sounds at my door, and I groan, pulling myself off of her. She huffs and goes to her hidey-hole in my closet. I just want to keep kissing her, but ignoring my visitor would be highly suspicious.

I brush my fingers through my hair and ask the room to air out Desireé's distinct sulphuric scent while I pad over and swing the door open.

Nicolai.

"Have you finished your midterm essay yet?" he asks, striding in without an invitation. I close the door and roll my eyes.

"Not even close," I say, sighing as I collapse on the bed. "I chose a subject that also happens to involve translating a buttload of Enochian."

He laughs. "I'm glad I chose something easy, then." He sits at my desk and glances at my open textbooks and the papers beside them for a moment, but he doesn't actually seem all too interested in them.

"What's up?" I ask, staring at the ceiling and wondering how it would look with a night sky drifting across. The room picks up on my thoughts and transforms, and I smile. No matter how much I do, my little slice of heaven will never cease to be cool.

Nicolai's response takes a moment, and I sit up to prick an eyebrow at him.

"We haven't talked about what happened between us," he says, then clears his throat. "The, uh, kiss." His face turns red. Maybe I should've done my essay over how Angels blush red even though our blood is gold. Then, his words absorb into my mind, and I'm thinking about kissing not him, but Desireé, and my cheeks react in kind.

"I mean," I say, "it was just a misunderstanding. Not a big deal, really."

He nods, but he still isn't looking at me. The answer seems to satisfy that question, but he still doesn't leave.

"Are you alright?" I ask.

His eyes finally pierce mine. "What's it like?" he asks. "Killing a demon?" That is not the question I'm expecting whatsoever. "One of the upperclassmen told me that, to get our wings, we have to kill a demon. I just…I don't know."

My heart twinges. The final exams are only in a couple more months, and first-term students will be sent to a base on Earth to kill captured demons and receive their wings. What if one of those demons were Desireé? I glance at my closet door for just an instant, and either he doesn't catch it, or he doesn't understand the significance of the look.

"It's kind of awful," I admit. "The first time it happened, I was hurt. Bad. I was only able to kill it because it was either do that or die." I chew my lip, considering my words carefully before continuing. "I don't know if I'd be able to do it how you guys have to. They look like people," I say, putting more emphasis on the final word. "They are people…" I stumble and correct, "Were. People."

When I spill the last sentence, I clam up. I've definitely said too much. If he discovers that I care about demons at all, it will bring others sniffing around. And there's plenty of sulphur for them to smell.

He just nods, though. "Thanks for your honesty." Then, he stands and walks to the door.

I stay on my bed, holding my breath. He turns around and looks at me.

"I hope you know that I still care about you," he says. "I know there's nothing romantic between us, and there never will be, but we're still friends, right?"

My eyes widen just a little. "Of course!"

He nods, then sets his jaw. "If any more demons come into the school, I want to come with you. I don't want you to have to kill one on your own." He sighs. "I don't know what I would do if you weren't here."

The whole exchange is getting too close to the secret in my closet. I look at the ground. "I'll see you in class," I say.

When I look up again, he's gone, and I can finally breathe again.

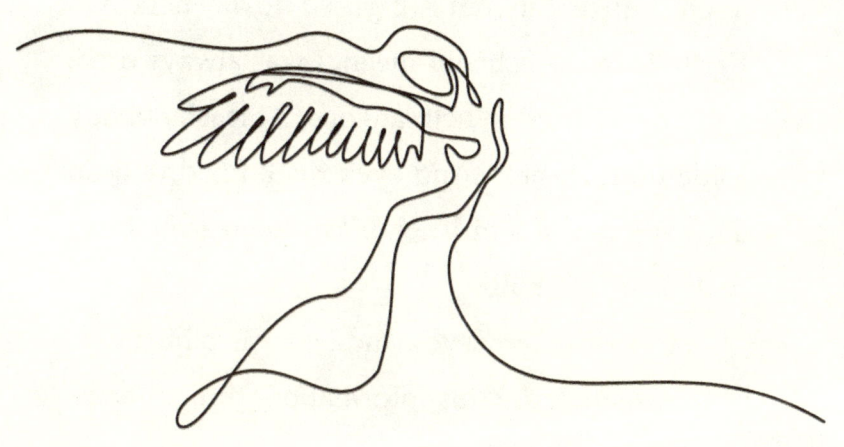

Chapter Twenty-Three

*I*t is rumored that Death has the power to exchange a
life for a life.

There it is.

The mystery I've been thirsting to solve. The
secret to all I've wondered about since I first de-
duced that my presence in Heaven doesn't make a
lot of sense. I double, triple, and quadruple check
the translation, but it remains the same.

I look at Desireé, who's sitting on my bed, legs
crossed beneath her as she watches a romantic
comedy and snacks on a bag of Cheetos.

I close the book and then my eyes.

Of course I'm not supposed to be here. On Earth, I was selfish and mean. I was always tired, and I never tried to help anyone. At least, nobody aside from Desireé. And even then, I hadn't been all that good of a girlfriend. I'm the reason we're both dead, after all.

Tears prick at my eyes, and I suck in a breath.

I cannot handle this information. I might actually vomit.

I should be in Hell. I should be a demon.

Desireé had been perfect. She'd done everything possible to make others' lives easier, and she'd been punished for it. Tortured. Destroyed. Broken down and built back up into a creature of darkness.

"Are you alright?" she asks, her voice distant as she seems to come back into the room from her movie. She does that sometimes, fades away so that her body is vacant for minutes or even hours at a time. Is that how she coped when she was tortured?

A sob bursts out of me.

She stands quickly, her chips spilling all over the

bed. She ignores them, though, and rushes over to me, taking my face gently in her hands.

"What's wrong?" she asks, her voice whispy, like it's made of smoke.

I try to speak, but the words just won't come out. This is wrong. I'm wrong. She's everything that's right in the universe. I wrap my arms around myself.

"I'm so sorry," I gasp as she strokes my hair. How is it that, although she's a demon who was tortured for years, she's the one who's now comforting me?

She kisses the top of my head.

"It's not your fault," she says. Her voice caresses me, and I want to float away with it.

"It is," I insist. "I came here, and you went there." I can't even say the word Hell. "I took your place. It's my fault you died, and it's my fault you got punished." I stifle my sobs against her sweatshirt, and she pets my hair.

"No," she insists. "It was my choice. I asked, and she agreed."

I shudder and look up, her face bleary through

my tears.

"What?" I whisper. I blink away my tears, only to find a devastated face looking down at me.

She has to lean down to press her forehead against mine.

"I made a deal," she says. Her voice isn't only wispy now, it's just the barest of breaths.

The wheels turn in my head. I close my eyes and clench my fists against her shirt. "No," I say. I'm not quite sure if I'm protesting or disagreeing. She has to be lying to make me feel better, right?

"I would do it again," she says, holding me tighter as I begin to shake.

"No," I moan. "You didn't. You can't…"

A memory fades in slowly. A meadow. A very human Desireé lying next to me, our fingers intertwined.

A woman's voice.

And after…

I love you, Avery.

"I can't…" I say, but I don't have the words for this. Why? How had this even happened? It shouldn't be allowed. Or possible. There are rules for this sort of thing.

"I don't regret it," she says, her voice strengthening with every word.

I bite my lip to keep another sob from wrenching out of me.

I am here because of Desireé. Because she loved me.

Loves me.

I shake my head, but I know it's true. That's the only explanation. How else could I have ended up here?

"I can't believe you would do that for me," I admit, sniffling. I can't decide how I feel. Confused, of course. But am I angry? Sad?

I take in a deep, shuddering breath, taking in her scent. Would I have done the same for her? Knowing that I could have all this?

I can't be certain that the answer is yes.

At that moment, though, before I can process, the door opens, and somebody gasps.

We've been discovered.

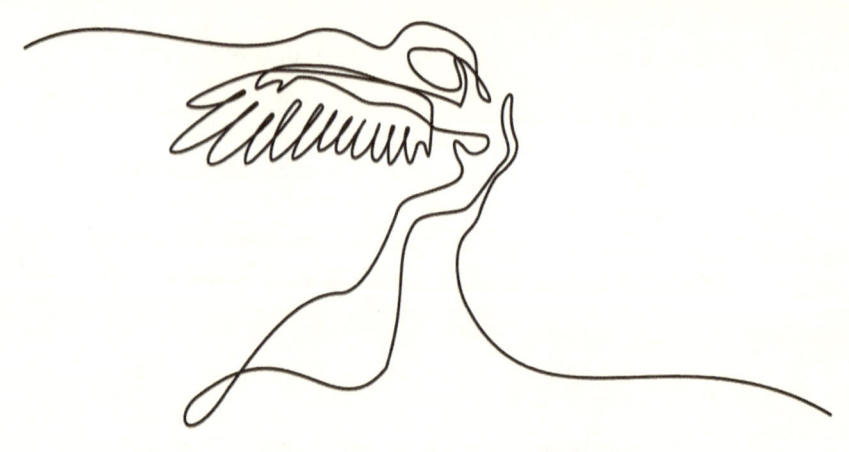

Chapter Twenty-Four

Azrael is at the door.

Her right hand covers her mouth, and her eyes are wide.

This moment is stuck, frozen. It's an eternity before anybody moves. When Azrael reaches for her weapon, a glistening ax, everything speeds up.

"No," I gasp out. Azrael's eyes are confused for just a moment, but she puts her attention right back on Desireé, whose body is blocking mine. I shove her out of the way and stand in front of her.

"Please," I beg, throwing my wings out to block Azrael from doing anything. My hands are shaking, and my eyes are still wet from tears.

Azrael's jaw ticks, but she lowers her weapon.

"Avery," she says slowly, "what has it done to you?"

I turn to Desireé, then back to Azrael. "She didn't do anything. She's not…" I search for the right words to explain what's going on, but all I come up with is "bad."

Azrael shakes her head. "Avery. Please. Try to see what you're saying."

A hand rests on my shoulder, and Azrael flinches like she's just been attacked. "Don't," Desireé breathes. "You'll only get hurt."

Azrael's eyes widen. "Avery, don't listen to whatever that creature is telling you. They have the power to alter your thoughts. Change your memories."

I don't take my eyes of Azrael. My heart races, and a few students have begun to trickle into the hall, peering and gaping over Azrael's shoulder.

"She's not going to hurt anyone," I say. "There's been a mistake. She's supposed to be here." A few students look at each other, murmuring.

"Avery," Azrael says, taking a gentle step toward me, "it's going to be alright."

I back up, but Desireé is stone-still behind me.

"It is?" I ask, glancing at Desireé, who merely gives me a piteous look before I turn back to the archangel.

"Yes," Azrael says, taking another step. I pull my hands back and search until Desireé wraps her fingers around mine. "I just need you to come to me. Nothing bad is going to happen. I promise."

I sigh with relief and look at Desireé once again. She smiles, but it doesn't reach her sad eyes.

It's all going to be okay. We'll figure this out. Azrael will help. I want to tell her all that, but she presses her lips to mine at the moment Azrael leaps forward and grabs me by the arm. I'm yanked away from Desireé, and when Azrael places a hand on my forehead, everything goes dark.

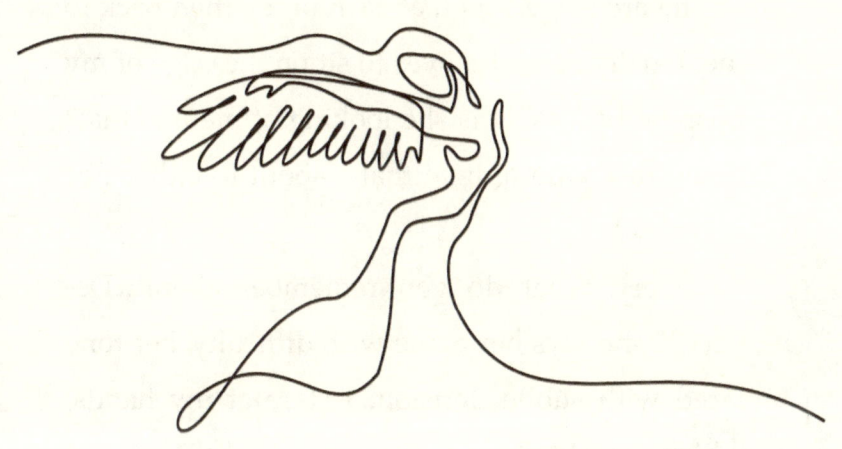

Chapter Twenty-Five

I open my eyes to find an arched marble ceiling that's far too bright.

It takes me a few moments of blinking and looking around to absorb that I'm back in the hospital wing.

"You're going to be alright," someone says to my left. I jerk my head over, and Gabriel and Azrael are both staring at me. It had been Gabriel's voice. My lip trembles, and I have to clench my jaw to stop it.

"What's going on?" I ask. I look around. "What happened to Desireé?"

The archangels look at each other, then back to me. Finally, Azrael moves to sit on the edge of my hospital bed. Why is she looking at me like that? Like I'm a wild animal that's about to either flee or attack?

"Avery, what do you remember about...Desireé?" she says her name with difficulty, her tone laced with subtle derision. I stare at my hands, which are folded in my lap.

"She and I were dating on Earth. She's the one that was in the car wreck with me." Out of the corner of my eye, Azrael and Gabriel give each other a significant look. I ignore it. How is it possible that I'm so tired right now? Even after sleeping for hours, I've never been drowsy in Heaven. What did Azrael do to me back in my room?

"Go on," Gabriel prods. He doesn't come any closer to me, though.

I sigh. I don't want to talk about this. Shouldn't they just trust me? "We were together for a long time. After we died..." I consider whether I should say this next part, but I have to tell them everything if they're to believe in her innocence. "She was there. With Cain."

One half of Azraels lips turn down. "That's odd," she admits. "Cain almost always meets with souls alone."

I nod. "I read that. But we were together. It was in a field, and then she left first. With Cain. The next thing I knew, I was waking up here." I shrug. "That's all I know. Except then, when the second attack came, she was there. I couldn't remember her until then. It was like everything was static, but when I saw her again, it all came back to me."

Azrael seems nervous and concerned. She tilts her head and rests a hand over mine.

"Avery," she says gently while Gabriel watches, "I know this is going to be difficult to believe, but some demons have powers. They have different abilities. And some..." She takes a deep breath before continuing, "Some are able to alter memories. They can put things there that weren't before. Things from your past life that don't quite add up, people that were never there...It's a power they use to create weakness in our ranks. I've seen it many times before."

I pull my hand away and glare at her.

"You don't know what you're talking about," I say.

Still, a tiny seed of doubt plants itself in my head, the smallest of invasions. Azrael would know, wouldn't she? I shake my head and bury it as far back as I can.

"I know this is difficult for you," Azrael says, and it really sounds like she cares. "Unfortunately, there's nothing I can do to fix this. The only way for this curse to be lifted is for you to believe in it."

I frown. That doesn't make a lot of sense. How could I possibly believe that Desireé isn't the girl I know her to be? The girl who grew up in the house up the road? The girl who was kind to me when bullies came after me in middle school? The girl who anxiously kissed me in the locker room after the pool closed for the night and we were finishing our lifeguarding shifts?

"Just think about it," Azrael says. Gabriel doesn't speak, and his mouth is a thin line. "You're free to return to your room, but I should warn you that most of the student body knows what happened

today. If you'd like, you are free to skip class tomorrow to recuperate and think about what I've
told you."

I nod. "Thanks," I say. I'm not sure if I mean it.

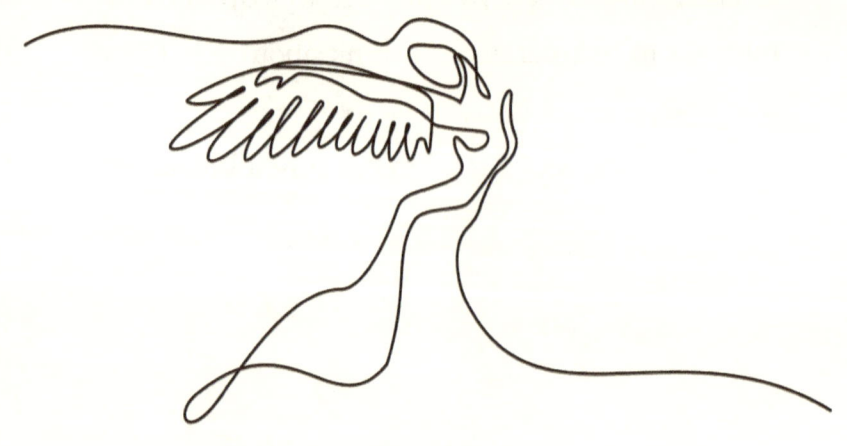

Chapter Twenty-Six

Desireé is not released, but she isn't dead. When Gabriel informs me of such with pity, I breathe a sigh of relief. There's still a chance she'll be okay. I have time to convince the angels to release her, to bring her to the light. She deserves to be here far more than I do.

Huỳnh and Gabe still sit with me at dinner, but they don't invite me out anymore. Instead, they give me wary looks. Maybe Azrael is making them spend time with me to force me out of my thoughts of Desireé. It doesn't work. They're uncomfortable around me, and it's obvious. I don't blame them.

I'd been caught consorting with a demon, and everyone things my mind has been altered.

Long after midterms, when the halls are buzzing about the final test for first-term students, I find Nicolai waiting at my door.

"Come in," I say when I catch him standing there. He steps inside, and I expect him to watch me out of the corner of his eyes, to be careful to not turn his back to me like everyone else.

He sits on my bed and leans back against my pillows casually, like he belongs here. The fact that he doesn't have wings means that he seems tiny on the expansive mattress that has grown to fit all of me.

"What do you want?" I ask, my mood sour. I've been reading as many books as I can about Cain, but I haven't found much more than the single sentence that ruined my life weeks ago. On the bright side, my Enochian assignments are coming back with excellent marks. With all the constant translating, I'm practically fluent in the language.

He raises an eyebrow, but he doesn't get up. "I just thought you could use a friend," he says, folding his arms behind his head like he owns the place.

"I have friends," I retaliate, but I'm not sure it's totally true. Although Huỳnh and Gabe still tolerate me, they clearly don't trust me in the slightest. Maybe I don't have friends anymore, but it's not like Nicolai has made anyone attempt to spend time with me lately, either. Nobody here trusts me, and I don't really blame them.

He sighs. "I'm not here to fight with you, Avery." He sits back up, his face going from cocky to concerned in an instant. "I've been watching you, to be honest."

This surprises me, and I take a step back. Is it possible that Nicolai is dangerous? Is he going to threaten me? Does he know about my research into Cain?

"I want to ask you about Death," he asks. The way he says it lets me know that he's not talking about the concept, but the person. The foreboding figure that people wonder about in the night.

"What about her?" I ask, sitting at my desk since he's taken up residence in my bed.

He looks at me, then looks at the door, then leans forward. When he speaks again, his voice is hushed, like he's afraid of being overheard.

"I don't think I'm supposed to be here," he says. "I heard what you said with…that girl. And I think, if you think she's supposed to be here, then it's possible that…" But he doesn't finish his sentence. His eyes dart to the door once again.

I laugh. I can't help it. The sound bursts out of me, and when I start, I can't stop. Tears spring to my eyes, and my shoulders shake. I can't breathe, so I guess it's a good thing I don't have to.

"What's so funny?" he asks, shooting to his feet.

I gasp for breath, more out of habit than necessity. "I thought I was the only one," I gasp out. His jaw drops.

"What are you talking about?" he asks, striding over to me. His shoulders are tense, and he crosses his arms.

I shake my head. The laughter is gone, but the tears are not. I shudder, and he puts a hand on my shoulder awkwardly.

"It's alright," he says. "Take your time."

I suck in a deep breath and try my best to quell the tears.

"This will be easier if I get my notes."

He nods.

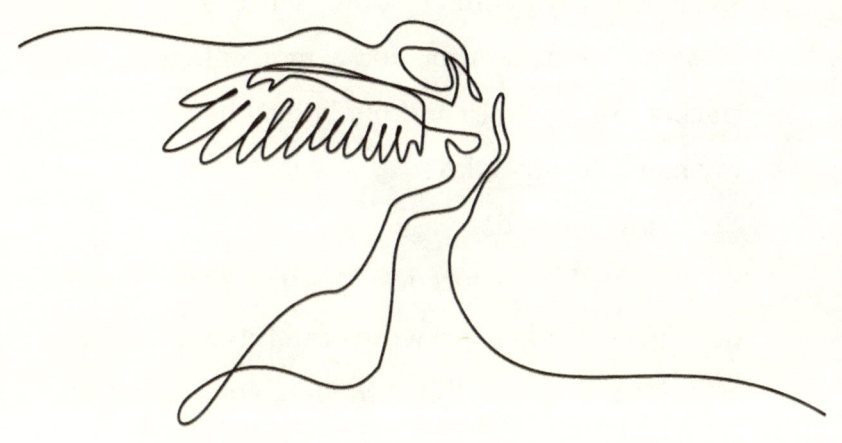

Chapter Twenty-Seven

"**I** want to speak with Cain," I say.

Azrael looks up from her desk in surprise, setting down the stack of papers in front of her.

"What?"

I look away from her eyes. I can't concentrate with her gaze on me. "I want to speak with Cain. Find out if what Des—" I stop myself from saying her name. It won't help my case. I still haven't seen her since she was taken from me, and I fear that I never will again. "The demon. I want to find out if what she said was a lie, like you say. And I think that Cain is the only way I can really lift the…" I struggle to say it, but I spit out "curse."

Azrael considers me for a moment, her eyes tracing over my face and my body. I have to force my hands to stay relaxed.

Finally, she nods.

"Alright," she concedes. "I will see what I can do." She considers her words carefully. "If the answer isn't what you think, though, you must drop these thoughts. They aren't good for you, and it will end badly if you aren't able to rid yourself of them."

At that, I clench my hands into fists, but I nod. "Of course," I say.

She smiles. "I'm glad you're beginning to see the light."

I look away. "Yeah, me too."

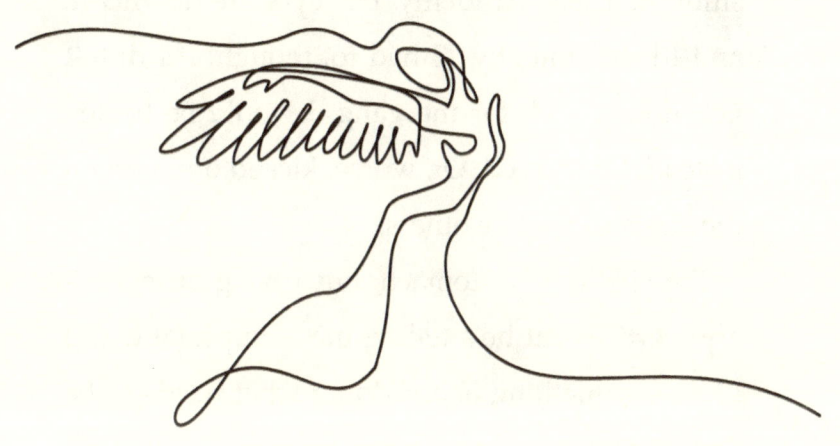

Chapter Twenty-Eight

While we wait for Cain's response, Nicolai tells me about his life.

He grew up in a huge city in Russia. Like me, he was poor. And, like me, he did what he had to in order to survive.

That's where the similarities end, though.

"I didn't want to hurt anybody," he breathes, sitting against the footboard of my bed while I lean against the headboard. There's a movie playing so that our conversation will be drowned out to any potential listening ears. I may be under suspicion, but that's no reason to compromise Nicolai's position in Theaa Academy. His eyes are downcast, and I listen intently. "I had to, though. If I didn't get money back for the gang, I would be beaten instead. Or starved. Or, worse, kicked out. Left on the street to die like others."

I'm sick to my stomach, but I hang on his every word. What he's telling me is important, and I know something about doing what needs to be done. I may not have broken anybody's kneecaps out, but I did steal from my friends' parents when there were slumber parties, small things like diamond earrings and silverware and crystal ashtrays. It took some practice, but I got good at determining what was valuable. I had to.

It eventually turned to worse things. Credit card fraud. Blackmail. I got really good at ruining marriages with false allegations if I wasn't given what I wanted. I may have never physically hurt anyone, but people were still hurt. Badly. The whole time, Dad didn't notice what was going on. He was too busy being passed-out drunk.

"If I'd known what came after," he said, his eyes sad, "I would have starved."

I nod. If I'd known that I would go to Hell, I would've just taken what life had given me. Maybe it could've gotten better for me if I hadn't done so much harm, but I was in too deep to stop. Now, though, it's so much worse than I could have imagined. Because I'm not the one who ended up in Hell, although I am the one who deserved it.

He scoots over and takes my hand in his, desperate for any form of comfort. I rub my thumb over the back of his hand, and it reminds me of the same motion I'd done to Desireé. Tears prick at my eyes. Her condition is my fault in every way. If I'd been better, tried harder, she would be here. Maybe we both would.

"In the end, I was killed by one of the targets," he says, his voice thick with emotion. "And after they threw me in the frozen river, they got Nadia." His fingers tighten on mine, and I ignore the tears streaming down his face.

"Nadia?" I ask gently.

He nods. "My twin sister."

I frown. I'd known the world could be a terrible place, but I never considered that the things Nicolai is telling me could happen in real life. It's like something out of a movie.

"She's the one who spoke to Cain on your behalf," I say, my words gentle.

He nods. "She must be. But I don't understand why I remember her. You said you didn't remember Desireé until you saw her again."

I shake my head. "I don't know. I really don't."

A knock at the door interrupts us, and we split apart. "Come in," I call.

Gabriel opens the door, and he looks uncomfortable being here. He hasn't quite warmed to me since the incident with Desireé.

"Cain is here," he says.

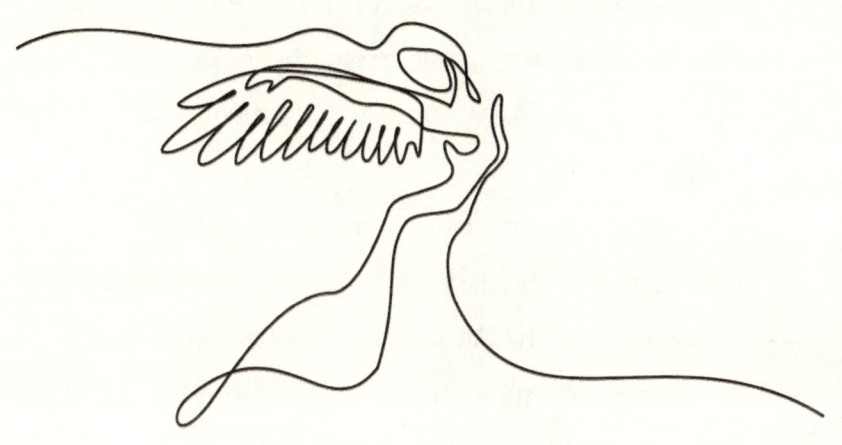

Chapter Twenty-Nine

Cain is not at all what I've been expecting.

I've been picturing a towering, shrouded figure in dark robes and carrying a scythe. Or a tall, muscular warrior queen with flowing golden hair.

Instead, I come face to face with a short, portly woman with skin as dark as the night sky and Earth-brown eyes that are wide as a baby deer. She has a mass of kinky hair that falls all the way to her waist, and her clothing is a simple pair of dark high-waisted jeans and a white t-shirt with a pale blue denim jacket.

When she smiles at me, I shiver. Getting a smile from Death is unsettling, to say the least.

"Avery," she says warmly. "It's nice to see you again."

I wrap my arms around myself, suddenly cold. Why the hell did I think I should be allowed to speak with Cain? As soon as I'm here with her, I know deep in my soul that she is more powerful than anyone I've ever met. Where the Archangels may be ancient, powerful beings, they can't control Death. They have no say over what happens when someone dies.

And Cain controls it completely.

She's more powerful than any of them. And I'm trapped in a room with her.

"No need to be afraid, Avery," she says, taking a seat in a big leather chair in the old-fashioned parlor where we've met. I didn't even know this room existed, although it's not too surprising. Theaa is huge, and I've only begun to scratch the surface of its secrets. "I know why you're here."

"You do?" I ask carefully. And what if I'm wrong about Desireé? What if it's all been one big trick?

I'm not sure I could bare the heartbreak.

She nods, then takes a sip of a drink that suddenly appears in her hand.

"Iced Mocha," she explains without prompting. "They're my absolute favorite. I was so excited when humans invented them."

I nod. I don't want to be the first to bring up my precarious situation at Theaa. I'd rather she say something. Mostly because, despite her diminutive frame, she is terrifying. Her whole body emanates power, and my wings shrink back, tightening close to my body.

"So, you want to talk about your girlfriend." She takes another sip of her drink.

I nod again. I have no idea what to say to her about this situation that she doesn't already know.

She shrugs. "I'm sorry, but she asked to switch places with you. There's nothing else I can do."

I suck in a breath, and tears prick at the corners of my eyes. "So it's true? I'm not supposed to be here?"

"Oh no, you're supposed to be here," Cain says. "Every person in Heaven or Hell is where they're supposed to be, because the decisions are mine to make and nobody else's." I'm about to protest, to ask why Desireé and I were switched if we had no say, but she stops me. "Sometimes, I listen to special cases." She narrows her eyes. "Sometimes."

I wait for her to continue, but she doesn't. It takes me three tries before I can convince my mouth to open and words to come out. "Nicolai, too?"

She nods. "Yes. His sister insisted that he was good at heart. I disagreed, but she insisted. So I did it."

I shake my head. This is all so much to process. The Angels were wrong. Desireé did nothing to me. "But why?"

She shrugs. "I was human once, too. And I did a terrible thing."

My eyes widen. "Your brother."

"Yes," she sighs. "Abel. He was a good person, too. For the most part. But one day, he lost his temper, and I defended myself." Her voice has gone distant. Although the memory is from thousands of years ago, she's acting like it was just yesterday. "I only meant to stop him. I didn't mean…"

She snaps back to attention, then clears her throat. "Anyway. He's doing great now. Heaven and all that. The Creator decided that I was to choose our fates. I thought I was being clever by saying that I would get to control Death." She hesitates.

I wait for her to continue. Whatever she has to say is worth more than any words that could come out of my mouth.

"This job…it takes a lot. And it's not easy. But I do what I can." She shrugs. "I'm only human, after all."

I sigh. Despite all her power, her age, her experience, I can sense that this last sentence is the truest of all. Beneath everything else, Cain is still human. She can see the nuances of good and evil, and she's the one who has to decide where each person falls.

"So what do I do?" I ask, my voice small. I may have wings and a magic sword, but I'm still just a seventeen-year-old screw-up.

She shrugs. "I only came here to tell you the truth. And have a conversation. It gets old talking to newly dead people all day every day."

My jaw drops. "So you're not gonna help me?

You're not gonna set things right so that Desireé is where she belongs?"

Her expression darkens. "Desireé is exactly where she belongs. That's what I'm trying to tell you. When I make my choice, that is what's supposed to happen. That's how it works. You may not have been a good person on Earth, what with all your swindling and life-ruining, but I put you here. Just like I put Nicolai here even though he's a murderer." She sets her jaw. "Now, if you'll excuse me, I have a job to do."

She sets her coffee on the side table, and, when I blink, she's gone.

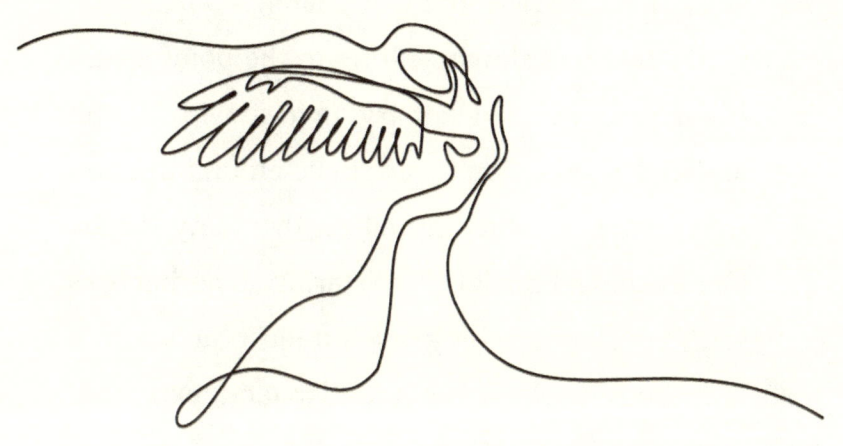

Chapter Thirty

The meeting had mostly been a waste of time, it seems. The only thing I know now that I didn't before is that I'm certain that Desireé didn't use any sort of magic on me. Back in my room, I confirm Nicolai's suspicions about his sister, and his face crumples into a thousand pieces.

We continue going through the days. If I'm where I'm supposed to be, then I can't convince the angels to release Desireé. She may be good, and she may deserve Heaven, but, according to Death herself, it's not where she belongs. The difference is maddening. And, without Cain on my side, I have no case for the Archangels.

My flying is slowly getting to the point where it's acceptable, and I stop trying to sit with Huỳnh and Gabe. They don't want to be around me, so I don't want to inflict myself on them any longer. One evening, I catch Huỳnh staring at me, her eyes sad. I consider reaching out, but I just can't.

Nobody could possibly understand, except, of course, Nicolai.

We tell each other about our lives.

About the people who sacrificed themselves for us.

In the mess hall one evening, we're eating our food and ignoring the chatter around us. "When I'd have sleepovers at her house, she'd make us pancakes with chocolate chips in the mornings," I tell him. The memory sits fondly in my head. It was like Desireé glowed in the morning light streaming in through the kitchen window, and her kisses had tasted like chocolate.

He smiles faintly. "Nadia always made sure I had enough blankets. The heat went out in our apartment, and we probably would have frozen to death without her." He frowns. "She didn't know where my money came from, only that it was enough to pay the landlord and keep us from starving. It would have killed her to know what I did." He pauses, and his eyes go sad. They do that a lot these days. "I guess it did that anyway."

I smile just a little back at him. It charms me that he'd kept his indiscretions from his older sister. "It's not your fault," I say. That's something we tell each other a lot, too. The one lie we tell each other. *It's not your fault she died.* Even though, for both of us, it was. We'd both been the causes of death.

Yet we'd been put in Heaven.

It's not fair.

Someone comes up to my right, and I glance up, surprised to find Huỳnh standing there.

"Hi, Avery," she says, the smallest of smiles on her face. She looks at Nicolai. "I'm Huỳnh," she says, sticking her hand out. "Third term."

He takes her hand in his. "Nicolai. First term." He gestures toward his back, empty of wings. "Obviously."

My shoulders are tense, but I don't ask about

Huỳnh's motivations. She seems uncomfortable enough as it is. She glances around and takes a seat.

She and Nicolai talk about boring stuff, classes and assignments and such, and I chime in with the occasional comment, but. I can't bring myself to be invested in what they're talking about.

"So," Huỳnh says slowly, "are you ready for the initiation test next week?" She glances at me, but then her eye contact goes back to Nicolai.

He shrugs. "I guess so. I mean, I kind of have to be, don't I?" He doesn't look ready, though. He hasn't said as much, but I know that the prospect that he might be killing an innocent person is getting to him. It makes sense. I'm terrified at the same idea.

Huỳnh nods slowly, then glances around, like she's checking to see if anyone is listening. They're not, of course. I stopped being interesting about a week after the incident with Desireé that half the school witnessed. They've moved well past that. Even Azrael is no longer wary of me since my meeting with Cain. Then, Huỳnh leans forward.

Out of habit, Nicolai and I do the same, although his face holds the same confused expression as the one I can feel forming on my own.

"Third terms are the ones who had to capture the demons for the initiation," she hisses, her eyes wide. Her fingers grip the table, the knuckles white as bone. She looks right at me when she continues. "Your demon is one of the ones there." She shakes her head, then takes a deep breath. "I looked over your notes for your essay. And I saw the note about Death being able to make switches."

I wait for her to ask the last question, the one that will reveal the truth, but she just watches me, waiting to see which of us will break first. My heart races at the thought that Desireé is locked in a cage somewhere, awaiting her death. And there's nothing I can do about it.

"It happened to me, too," Nicolai mumbles, and her head snaps toward him. Her eyes go even wider, which I hadn't realized was even possible. They're practically popping out of her skull. "My sister. She was going to be here, not me, but Death switched us."

Huỳnh takes a moment to process this, then sighs. Her eyes go back to a reasonable size as she leans back. "Wow," she whispers. She wraps her arms around herself as if she's cold or something. "Wow," she says again.

After a few moments of silence while she processes this, I say, "It's true. Cain told me that she switched Desireé and I when we died." I'm almost to the point where I can say that without my voice shaking, although I stumble over her name. She's going to die. For real this time. She'll be well and truly gone. Because of me. *Again*.

Huỳnh grits her teeth. "If that's true," she says slowly, "then maybe there's something we can do." Her voice wavers, and she looks around like someone might be listening in.

My eyes widen. "What are you talking about?"

She shakes her head. "Not here. I'll meet at your room after dinner."

I nod. This conversation has already gotten into dangerous territory. If someone were to hear us, we could all be in big trouble. What type of trouble do Angels get in, though? I can't imagine that it's anything simple.

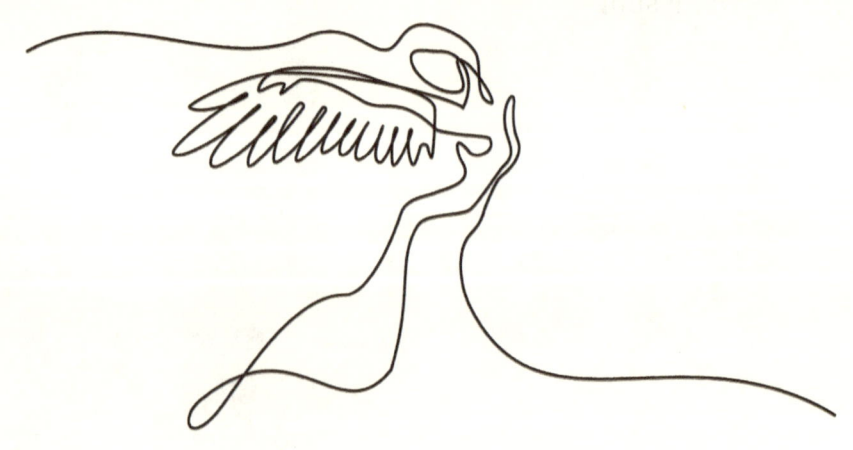

Chapter Thirty-One

We stay up all night every night going over the plan. We're extremely limited on what we know, but when Gabe finally comes around and joins us, his insight as a fourth-term student is invaluable.

It has to go perfectly. If every single step doesn't go according to plan, then we'll be screwed.

When the day of the test finally arrives, I can't help but clench my teeth. What if everything goes wrong? What if our plan is actually a disaster?

According to Gabe, we could be exiled. I don't ask him to elaborate what happens when someone is exiled from Heaven. It can't be pleasant.

All first-term students meet in the hospital wing, the same place where we first arrived. It's strange being back here. I almost expect the windows to explode and a hoard of demons to attack, but nothing happens.

"Remember," Azrael says to the fifty or so of us standing in a line, "on Earth, none of us will have wings. We look just like regular humans as to blend in, but you are not to leave the grounds of the facility. You are not cleared for regular patrols, and we are only going to be on Earth for your exams." I frown at the word "exams," like it's just some normal test rather than angel-endorsed murder. Although I already have my sword and wings, I'm still supposed to kill a demon. I can't imagine having to kill someone now, knowing that there's a human buried deep inside.

I expect a heavenly light to envelope us, maybe a breeze, but I simply blink, and everything is dark.

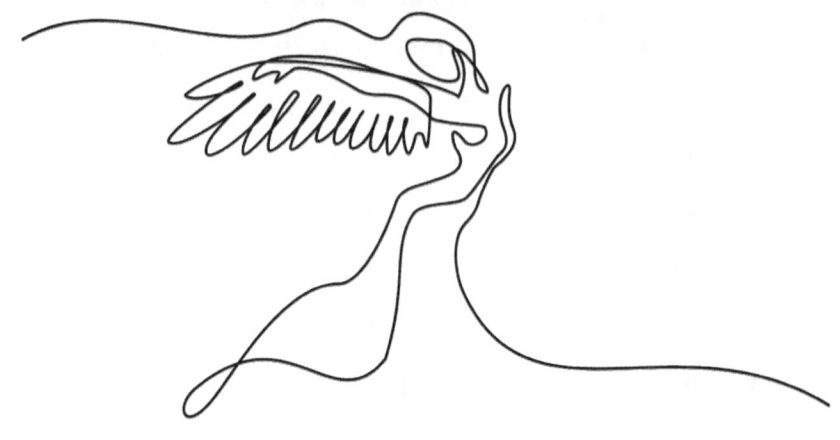

Chapter Thirty-Two

It takes my eyes a moment to adjust. I have to blink a few times, and the air is grimy and damp. I cough, hacking up as much of the stale air as possible. I don't want any of it in my system. I guess I just won't breathe while I'm here. Although she'd warned us about it, I still feel naked without my wings.

A line of cages stands before me, rows and rows. There's one demon per cage, and, while their features differ in many ways, they all have the same basic structure. Some sort of wings, although some are black bird wings with disintegrating feathers or impish insect wings. Horns, some spiral like Desireé's, some straight up, some long, some short. And a tail, mostly long and thin with a tuft of hair at the end, but some are more like cat or wolf tails, and I even spot one rat-like tail.

We're still standing in a line, and Azrael begins to call our names, just like she said she would. I'm third on the list.

"Avery," she says. "Choose your demon."

I have to keep myself from sucking in a breath, lest I choke on the rancid Earth air again. This is just like Gabe and Huỳnh said. We each choose from hundreds of demons. Once everyone has chosen, the ceremony begins. I make eye contact with Azrael. "I know exactly which one I'm going to kill. Where is it?"

Azrael smiles at me, that same pity on her face once again. I wish I could fault her for not believing in Desireé, but she's an Angel. One of the original Archangels. Of course she's not going to trust a demon. She points off to the right, and I stride confidently to the dim corner.

Immediately, I recognize the form crouched in

the corner, although she no longer has the confidence she'd slowly gained whilst hiding in my room with me. Instead, she's hunched over, her arms wrapped around her knees, her face tucked in. Her back is to me, but I have every one of her features memorized. Her wings, her horns, her hair, her tail, her hands…I grit my teeth. Around her wrists is a delicate silver chain. The skin underneath is rubbed raw, although the extent of the damage is difficult to tell past her pitch-black skin.

"Look at me," I command. I can still feel Azrael's eyes on me. I can't do anything for the plan until she's moved on.

Slowly, Desireé's head turns, and her eyes widen. She scrambles over to me desperately, and, despite how much it kills me, I sneer. "You thought you could trick me," I say, my voice just loud enough to be heard at the line, but not too loud as to sound fake. "Now, you're going to get exactly what you deserve."

She cringes at my words, her eyes filled with hurt. My heart tears in two at the sight.

Trust me, I mouth, and her eyes widen just a little. She gives me the subtlest of nods, and some of the tension lifts from my shoulders. She's going to have to believe in me for just a little bit if this plan is to work.

"Beatrice," Azrael calls.

It's time for step two.

While Azrael is looking away, I whisper as quietly as possible, "Give me your hands."

Desireé looks at the line of students and then back to me.

"Hurry," I say. "We don't have a lot of time."

She comes closer to me, lifting her hands to the bars.

"You can create illusions, right?" I ask, working while I speak. She nods the tiniest bit. I'm glad that we're obscured by darkness. Otherwise, my actions would be obvious to anyone paying attention. I relay the plan to Desireé, my voice the barest of breaths. I can't risk being overheard.

When I'm finished, Desireés blood-red lips tilt up in the tiniest smile.

"We won't be able to see each other again, will we?" she asks. Her eyebrows are tilted up in sadness. I shake my head.

"No. This is the end."

She takes my hand gently and glances behind me to make sure we aren't being watched. Then, she presses her lips to my palm. A sharp pain slices just barely into the skin from one of her claws, and I flinch, but I keep the gentle smile on my face. When I take my hand back, I clench my fingers over the injury so that nobody sees me bleeding. Even on Earth, my blood shines golden.

"Everything will be alright," I say. Then, after a pause, "And thank you. What you did for me is something I will never stop being grateful for. You were always better than me, and you deserved better."

She shakes her head and laughs under her breath. "I love you, Avery," she says, like it's just that simple. I'm about to respond in kind, but Azrael calls us to attention.

It's time.

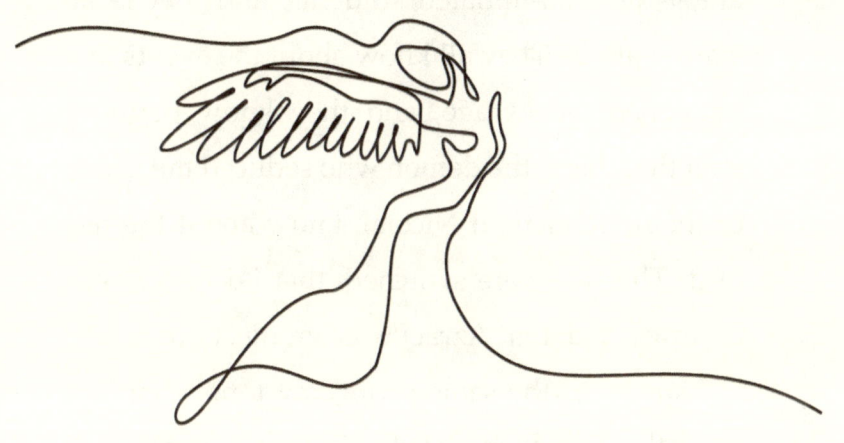

Chapter Thirty-Three

This is the end. Everyone is watching me. Three demons are dead, and I can't help but stare at the spot where they used to be. As each new angel finishes the job, they take the silver chains and wrap them around their wrists. A sort of trophy. I'm going to be sick.

I can't be sick. I have to pretend that everything is alright. That I am completely okay with what's going on right now, even if it makes me want to vomit.

Desireé stands before me, kneeling in the binding circle on the ground. There's an entire circle of angels and un-initiated students, and they're all staring at me. They all know about the events that happened weeks ago, and they know perfectly well that this is the demon who seduced me. None of them, other than Nicolai, know about the rest of it. That we were switched, that I'd never been brainwashed, that Azrael was wrong about her.

I spout off the same script, my tongue curling over the Enochian words. Desireé doesn't look up at me. The sight of her on the ground has my stomach roiling. I take her very solid hand in mine, drawing it up and scraping a claw over my palm. The golden blood flows out, just like it had with everyone else. First blood is what summons our weapons, although I only do it because of the ceremony. I already have my sword in its crystal sheath at my side.

I tilt her chin up to face me, and her black eyes stare back. I try to find any trace that the plan is going right, but I only have to have faith. Because if I'm wrong, she's going to die. "It's okay," she whispers, a tear falling from her face. Her voice is just a little wrong. It's not quite hers.

"You aren't the girl I love," I say, trying to project confidence into my voice. With that, I draw my sword and plunge it into her heart. She screams, just like every other demon had, and the sound burns into my ears. Tears prick at my eyes. I cannot show weakness. I watch as the life leaves her eyes, and she reaches a hand toward me as she disintegrates.

I suck in a breath of poisonous Earth air, and let out a shuddering breath. After sifting through the ashes on the ground, I lift the chain for all to see and wrap it around my wrist.

I may have already had wings and a sword before this, but now, my initiation is complete. I'm no longer a term one student.

I'm officially an angel.

And Desireè is gone. Really gone.

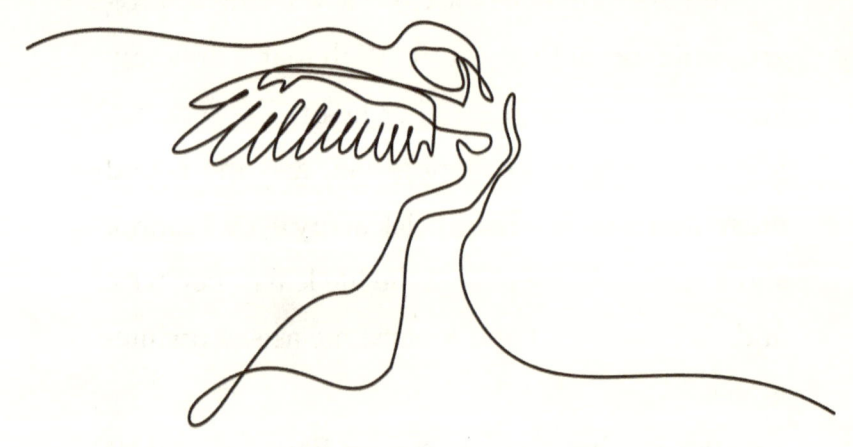

Chapter Thirty-Four

Although Nicolai hesitates to kill the demon in front of him, he does it anyway, his jaw tight and eyes glazed over. Is this how he used to kill people to survive? Did he disassociate just to get the job done?

I don't want to think too much about it.

"Well done," Gabriel says, clapping a hand on my shoulder. "Honestly, I wasn't sure you would do it."

I nod. "I had to." It's not technically a lie. I did what I had to.

When everyone is finished, we arrive back in

Heaven. Azrael goes around and heals everyone's wounds, and she spends an extra moment to grin at me. "I knew you'd be able to fight the curse," she said. "You're strong. One of the strongest recruits I've met."

I give one short nod.

She tilts her head. "I think you should get some rest. You've had a difficult term. More difficult than most students."

I sigh with relief. "Thank you," I say.

When I get back up to my room, I undress and change into my pajamas. When I'm about to toss my uniform blazer on the floor, though, something in the pocket stops me. A small slip of paper.

I unfold it, and it's hastily scrawled.

Avery,

I will be long gone by the time you read this.

I love you.

I'm okay.

I will find you again.

Desireé

My hands shake, and I read it over and over again. She's okay. She must be. She wouldn't have given me this note if she hadn't been certain that the plan would work. That she would be able to create an illusion version of herself and escape since I removed the binding silver chain from her wrists back at the cage. The chain only an angel could remove.

I walk into my closet and climb into the hiding space I'd created for her. After she'd been taken, I'd refused to get rid of it. I curl up on the twin-sized bed, staring at the ceiling. Until now, I haven't so much as moved the fake wall to look inside, and, although weeks have passed, her scent envelopes me like I'm wrapped in her arms. I stare at the ceiling, and my name is etched into the wood, burned in by her claws over and over again.

She has to be alright. Or, as alright as she can be now that she's returned to Daemaac Academy. Although we'd spent all our brief time together that we could, she'd never actually elaborated on what Daemaac Academy is like. It must be truly terrible if she'd kept it from me.

I smile at my name and wrap myself in her blankets, imagining that she's asleep next to me. Tears drip from my eyes, down my face, and onto the bed. At least she's still alive. She'd merely created an illusion for the angels' sake. Still, I go over it in my head again and again. The way it had looked so much like her that I hesitated. The way she'd reached up to me.

I fall asleep in the cubby, wrapped in her smell. I hope it never goes away. And, because I hope, and it's my room, it won't.

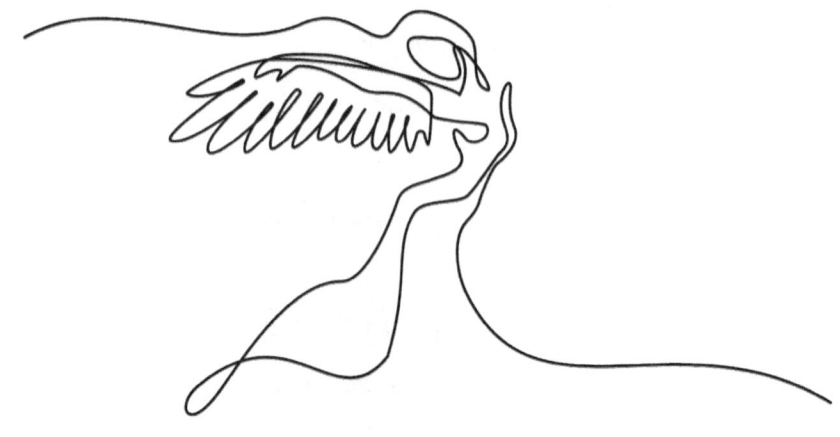

Chapter Thirty-Five

Now that we've finished our first term, we're given a special treat that nobody warned me about. All first term students are brought back to the infirmary, and when we blink, we're somewhere else.

It's a city, but nothing like the cities I've seen in real life or on TV. The buildings are spires that spear through the sky, all pristine gold and glass. There are shops of sorts, but there are very few employees. Mostly, it seems like everything is automated, kind of like my room had been.

When I finish gaping upwards in the square

we've appeared in, I look down to find that the streets are, in fact, paved with gold. Trees that are white as bone line the sidewalks, although there are no cars in sight to be on the road. Everyone has wings, and everyone is beautiful. Some are flying from place to place, and I spot a couple strolling through a park across the street, and they kiss lightly as they walk past.

"I'd like you all to meet back here in four hours," Azrael says, a grin smattered across her face. Her eyes are alight with excitement. "Oh, and don't fall off the edges. None of you have learned to use your wings yet."

I'm still gaping, and I raise my hand like we're still in a classroom. "What is this place?" I ask, although I'm too distracted by all the beauty to actually make eye contact with Azrael.

Her eyes twinkle. "This is Heaven," she says, then shrugs. "Well, another tiny piece of Heaven."

My breath catches, and I smile slowly. Heaven. Exactly how it should be. No demon attacks, no talk of war, no classes. Just joy and streets lined with gold.

As I see another couple tumbling through the sky above, locked in a gorgeous aerial dance, my heart drops.

It may be Heaven, but it's not how it should be. Not without Desireé by my side.

I think back on the note that's hidden in her cubby, the note I read to myself over and over again.

I will find you, I promise in my head. *We will be together again.*

KATE HALL is a full time traveler, dog owner, artist, wife, and reader. She believes in wild things like love, magic, and basic human decency. Some of her least favorite things include selfish people, eating fish, and tornados. *Sign up for her mailing list for exclusive access to free short stories!*

www.KateHallBooks.com

Twitter @KateHallAuthor

Instagram @KateHallAuthor

Books By Kate Hall

From the world of THE ACADEMY:
Smoke and Mist
Ignite the Mountain

ANGEL ACADEMY
Angel Academy
Clandestine Angel
Renegade Angel

GINGER HILLS
The Girl in the Lake
The Girl Who Won't Drown
The Girls Down Below

VAMPIRE HUNTER CHRONICLES
Night Academy
Deadly Academy
Final Academy

SOUTHERN WITCHES
Southern Charms
Southern Spells
Southern Neromancy